THE RELUCTANT RANCHER

Joann Baker &Patricia Mason

ISBN-10:0615880193
ISBN-13:978-061588098

DEDICATION

This book is dedicated to the two women
who give us unconditional love, now and forever,
our mothers: Maude Baker and Norma Hopkins

ACKNOWLEDGMENTS

Some say the journey of a thousand
miles begins with a single step.

Writers say a New York Times Best Seller
begins with a darn good idea.

Here's to having that idea sooner rather than later.

CHAPTER ONE

Mary Carter finished her exam of the two month old infant and handed the beautiful baby girl back to her mother. "She's doing great, Jennifer, but how's Mommy?" A registered nurse and the owner of a home health agency, she had provided assistance after her best friend had come down with a nasty case of the flu just days after giving birth. Today marked her last official visit to the Talbot household.

"I'm fine," Jennifer assured her. "But I don't know how I would have coped if you hadn't been here, especially during those first few weeks."

Mary smiled and packed away her stethoscope in an old-fashioned black doctor's bag that Jennifer had given her as a present last Christmas. Moving to Fiddler Creek, Wyoming, had proven to be the best thing she had ever done. Not only did she have her best friend nearby, but the town and its people felt like home. It would be the end of her world if she had to leave.

She tried to push her worries to the back of her mind as she watched Jennifer smile and coo at her daughter as she placed the baby back in her wooden crib. She knew her business would succeed, but she needed an influx of money–and fast. And her plan to get that money literally had her shaking in her boots.

"Much as I love you and Jessica, I did come here with an ulterior motive." Mary grimaced as she spoke. "My car is in the shop again and I need to borrow yours to drive out to the Tanner ranch."

"The Tanner ranch!" Jennifer exclaimed loudly, startling the drowsy infant. "Whatever for?"

"Why do you think? Money." She continued quickly before Jennifer could utter the words Mary knew she wanted to say. "I don't have much of a choice. The banks won't loan me money and my application has been with the Small Business Administration for months now. My hands are tied. If I don't get some working capital, and soon, I'll be out on the street and everyone who works for me will be out of a job."

Even though patients were plentiful, reimbursement from insurance companies came in slowly. And with all of the start-up costs inherent to a new business, some weeks she barely made payroll. She couldn't remember the last time she'd received a full paycheck. To make matters even worse, last week her landlord had called and raised the rent on her office building. No way did she have the money to pay more rent. Because of her cash flow problems, the small space already doubled as her office and home. Thank goodness it had a small efficiency apartment upstairs.

The higher rent, intermittent payments, and unexpected expenses meant taking out a loan until the business began operating deeply in the black, something Mary predicted happening in just under a year. Yesterday the banker at United Trust had politely, but firmly, put paid to the idea of a conventional business loan. So that left only one alternative–Luke Tanner, the richest man in the valley.

"Mary, are you sure you want to ask Luke? You know how he gets when people ask him for things." Jennifer's expression said it all. Many good citizens of Fiddler Creek had felt the sting of the rancher's razor sharp tongue after approaching him for help with one community project or the other. When it came to charity, Luke really only tolerated Mark, Jennifer's husband, and his notorious do-good deeds.

"Remember the summer camp for kids?"

"Don't I ever?" Last year the reclusive rancher had grudgingly allowed the county to run a camp for underprivileged kids on an unused parcel of the Circle T. Far away from the main house. When the counselor had suggested Luke come out and give riding lessons he'd refused, saying he had better things to do than teach a bunch of smart-assed juvenile delinquents how to be horse thieves.

It said something, though not much, that the man allowed the county to use the land free of charge.

And loaned his cowboys to give riding lessons. But then, maybe the rich rancher just needed a tax write-off. Not that her proposition could be deemed a charity case, Mary thought quickly. Hers was a legitimate business venture, which would prove very lucrative given time. But time was a luxury she could ill afford.

Mary's stomach tightened into knots just contemplating asking the meanest, orneriest man in the county for a big chuck of change. And based on what? The fact that she, Mary Carter, thought she deserved it? She had never thought herself worthy of anything in her life, never 'up to standard'. She always felt someone prettier or smarter or just plain better always lurked in the shadows ready to step into her shoes.

Despite Mark's steadfast friendship with the man and the small amount of evidence to the contrary, Luke Tanner was a mean son-of-a-bitch by anyone's standards. Plus it didn't help matters that she had a full-blown crush on the hard-nosed rancher.

She sighed, remembering how disappointed she'd been last summer on the rare occasions Luke had graced the camp with his presence. Naturally, he'd overlooked her just like most every other man ever had. Not that she'd expected fireworks and rockets and an instant proposal of marriage.

She'd long ago accepted the fact that she would never be one of those small, dainty women that everyone seemed to find so attractive. She stood five-foot-five in her stocking feet and carried more weight on her frame than recommended by the height and weight charts. As she'd gotten older, she had finally found a semblance of peace with her size, but not before spending many long, lonely years.

Not that she could be called a slouch in the romance department by any means. In fact, before she moved to Fiddler Creek she'd had a very active social life. Even though she didn't have the waif-like figure of a runway model, Mary wasn't an unattractive woman. Regardless of what the media touted, there were men out there who loved big, beautiful women. She'd had her share of romantic adventures, but they had been just that-adventures. Nothing that ever made her long to stay around for the happily-ever-after, or even for the night. She, like every other woman in the world, large or small, just wanted to meet the man who made her feel beautiful and special.

But it would have been nice if there had been some flicker of awareness–and dare she even hope–attraction from Luke Tanner. She hadn't even told Jennifer about her feelings for the man. Her friend would have ranted and raved, saying Mary deserved someone better. But Mary knew who she wanted, not who she deserved. But that, too, was just some hopeless, romantic fantasy. Sinfully rich, Luke Tanner could have any woman he wanted, and that woman would never be someone like Mary. It never was.

"Oh, Mary, I didn't know things were so bad. You know Mark and I would help if we could."

Jennifer's soft voice broke into her musings and she smiled, glad for the distraction. That was enough wallowing in self-pity for one day. "I know. But you have the boys and this little one to think of."

Mary moved across the room, pulling back the pink gingham curtains to look outside. Jennifer and Mark's house overlooked the valley floor giving her a spectacular view of Fiddler Creek. Again, she thought what a wonderful place she'd found to live and how heartbroken she'd be if she had to leave. For the first time in her life, she finally felt at home, at peace with herself. Not judged on anything but her skills and abilities.

Her childhood had been a constant state of upheaval with a military father who had been transferred every few years. Her brothers and sisters had relished the vagabond lifestyle, but not Mary. The constant moving combined with a weight problem had made her childhood difficult. Made it hard for her to join in, be one of the 'crowd'. She had always longed for a place of her own. A place to call home. Now she'd found it.

"Let Mark talk to Luke," Jennifer urged. "You know they're friends."

Mary let the curtain drop back into place and joined her friend at the door. "That's not a good idea, Jennifer. If he says no, I don't want this to come between your family and Mr. Tanner. I'm a big girl and I can take care of this myself."

Despite his hard-as-nails reputation, both women knew Luke Tanner provided the house the Talbots lived in free of charge and made generous–and what he thought to be anonymous donations which ensured Mark received his salary from the church every month.

With one last look at the now sleeping infant, the women tiptoed from the room. Mary took note of her friends drooping shoulders. "You look like you could use a nap. While you're sleeping I'll whip up a batch of my world famous, double-fudge, chocolate brownies."

"Ummm."

Mary laughed at her friend's groan at the mention of the calorie-laden treat. Both women knew Jennifer would not be able to resist the chocolate temptation. Or change Mary's mind about going to the Circle T.

Luke Tanner swiped at the stray lock of hair that had fallen across his brow. Picking up a precut post from the pile stacked neatly against the corral, he walked to the fence line. He frowned as he caught sight of an old pickup making its way up the long winding road that led to his ranch.

With an approving nod he noted the slight dust trail the truck kicked up. Released from the bitter cold of winter, the rich Wyoming soil prepared itself for the renewal of life once again.

But his eyes narrowed as he watched the truck approach. Because of his less-than-welcoming reputation, not many people deliberately made their way to the Circle T. He could afford to be that way, being one of the richest men in Wyoming and *the* richest man in the little town of Fiddler Creek. Heaving the post in place, he packed the soil firmly around the treated lumber with the heel of his work-worn cowboy boot.

Who knew what the visitor wanted this time? When someone came to call it usually meant he should get out his checkbook and make a donation to the latest fund-raiser, offer the use of his land for some community hoopla, or hire some down-and-out drifter looking for a job. Always something. No one ever came to see him, to see what they could do for him. He laughed bitterly. The self-pitying thoughts were not his usual style but lately he'd been unable to stop them. He'd felt out of sorts a lot lately. Used. Taken for granted. Put upon.

Being completely honest with himself, he'd felt that way since his ex-wife, Debbie, had walked out on him two years ago on their wedding night. Time hadn't healed that hurt; he'd just managed to bury it deeper inside.

As the truck passed close enough for him to see its make and model, his frown deepened. The old Chevy belonged to his friend, Mark Talbot, but Mark wasn't at the wheel. His friend had moved his new bride to Fiddler Creek more than ten years ago to serve as pastor of one of the many churches in Fiddler Creek. He was one of the few men in Lincoln County that Luke considered a close, personal friend and their friendship was incongruous at best–the renegade and the preacher. Who would have thought?

Peering closer, he still couldn't make out the driver. Hell, they could be male or female underneath the oversized coat they wore. He'd bet the ranch that no woman's high heeled shoe pressed against the accelerator. His full lips quirked upward in a self-derisive smile. Luke had a lot of money and some even used the term 'rich as sin' when describing him. However, the face in his mirror did not belong to a handsome man. He would even go so far as to describe himself as dog ugly. That, combined with his gruff attitude, made most females shy away from any close contact with him.

He sighed in resignation, set one last post in place and headed for the house. No doubt he was about to be saddled with another of Mark's good deeds. He shook his head in exasperation at what he considered his friend's fool-heartedness in seeing the best in everyone. Even though Mark never directly asked for his help, somehow, some way, Luke always found himself in the middle of the preacher's latest Good Samaritan cause.

"Who the hell are you and what are you doing on my land?"

The shock of the deep male voice held Mary immobile for several seconds. She turned slowly, facing the man she had come to see. But if the sound of his voice had shocked her, the sight of the man stunned her. Mary had seen Luke Tanner on several occasions but she had never been this up close and personal. A mountain of a man, she had to look up to see his face. A long way up. With genuine feminine appreciation she realized that Luke Tanner would stand at least six-foot-four in his stocking feet. His shoulders were broad and sturdy, their huge mass emphasized by the flannel-lined denim work jacket he wore. His large size made her, Mary Carter, feel small and dainty.

A patch of dark, curling hair peeked out from the neckline of his blue plaid western shirt and her stomach quivered at the tantalizing glimpse of his permanently sun-darkened chest. Her gaze fell, drinking in the sight of his strong, muscular legs. Whitewashed jeans clung lovingly to every male sinew. Even though his waist could never be called slim, it was in perfect proportion to his size. To Mary, he was a fine looking man.

With great reluctance, she tore her gaze away, taking in the rest of his sun-bronzed features–his frowning forehead, his beard-roughened jaw, and his crooked nose. Immediately his eyes captured her attention. My goodness, she had never seen such incredible eyes. Green as the mountain grass after the first spring rain and surrounded by lashes a woman would die for.

Mary shivered, more in reaction to this potently virile male than from the cold seeping beneath her coat.

"Are you deaf? I asked you a question, woman." The voice roared again, more impatient than before.

"I'm sorry." She mumbled the apology absently, still bemused by her first up close look at the man. Her crush had just been thrown into overdrive. She offered him a gloved hand. "Mr. Tanner, I'm Mary Carter, a friend of Jennifer and Mark Talbot. I called yesterday and set up an appointment to talk to you."

Mary saw the narrowing of his eyes as he shook her hand. She returned his stare, her eyes steady even though she blushed and wanted to look away.

"You must have spoken with my grandfather. What is it this time? I've given to the Red Cross and the Little League. Are you here to collect for the Save the Whales Campaign? Because if you are, honey, I'm telling you it's a lost cause. To the best of my knowledge, no whale has ever been stranded in Fiddler Creek."

The cold sarcasm in the rancher's voice was exactly what she'd expected. She'd know he'd be hardnosed, but her self-doubts rose. Was he judging her on how she looked? If she'd been a long-legged blonde would he have smiled and welcomed her with open arms?

Open arms. My, oh my, wouldn't that be something? She would bet her next paycheck that would be something any woman would want to remember.

She scolded herself for her lack of self-confidence. Now was not the time to let her insecurities surface. She had a chance to make a difference in her life and she would not let one stubborn cowboy stand in her way. She felt her temper rise as he continued to stare at her.

Luke Tanner was not God's gift to women by anyone's standards. His features were rough hewn and rawboned and he would never grace the cover of GQ any more than she'd be selected as a cover girl for Cosmo. She wanted so badly to pick up her briefcase, march back to Mark's truck and drive away from the Circle T and the obnoxious man standing before her. Only the thought of the six part-time nurses on her payroll prevented her from hightailing it back to town as fast as she could.

"I'm not here to collect for any charity, even though it wouldn't hurt you to donate to Save the Whales," she couldn't resist adding, her temper swelling several more degrees. He looked totally bored. She took a calming breath and continued before losing her nerve. If she was going to be dismissed out of hand, she might as well go for broke. "You see, Mr. Tanner, I'm a nurse and–"

"I suppose you'll do." Luke cut her off. "I don't know what my grandfather told you concerning the job, but it's yours. Follow me." He strode up the steps leading to the sprawling ranch house.

"Wait a minute." She put a restraining hand on his arm as he passed, earning herself a fierce glare in return.

"What is it now? I'm a very busy man."

Mary almost lost her nerve. Almost. "I didn't come here about a job. I came here to ask for a loan."

He stopped abruptly. "I am not your local ATM, darling," he drawled, contempt evident in every line of his craggy face.

"I never thought you were, *sugar*," she replied testily, taking a deep breath. "And believe me, if I had any alternative other than coming to you, Mr. Tanner, I'd have taken it." She knew her mocking tone rolled off him like water on a duck's back but she'd never liked the casual endearments men threw out like bathwater. When someone called her darling, she wanted it to mean something.

"I called yesterday to speak with you. The man who made the appointment said nothing about interviewing for a job."

The big man sighed and shook his head. She hid her smile, wondering if his relative sometimes gave him hell on occasion.

"Since my grandfather saw fit to make you an appointment, it's only fitting he be included in your little presentation. You can pitch your business plan over dinner. Welcome to the Circle T, sweetcakes."

Irritation swelled at the taunt, but she held her temper as she tried to keep up with his long-legged strides. Her mind whirled.

What had just happened?

Did he need a nurse or did she present her plan? He didn't look sick. In fact, he looked like an incredibly healthy male specimen. A fine specimen indeed, she thought, catching sight of the well-worn denims pulling tight over his firm butt and muscular legs as he climbed the front porch steps. Whoa, Mary, she chided herself. She couldn't let herself think about her growing attraction to this man. She had to think of her future and the future of her business.

She'd show the arrogant rancher she could make him money. Not a lot, but a tidy enough sum for him to consider financing her business for the next year or two. A five-year projection of income and expenses for her agency lay in her briefcase. Experts were predicting that the healthcare industry would be the wave of the future and she wanted to ride that crest to the top. Now she just had to convince the reluctant rancher.

Chanting *now or never* under her breath, she hurried to catch up with the fast disappearing man.

Once inside the beautiful home, she followed the sound of his booted footsteps. As she passed through the living room, she faltered and came to a complete stop.

The large room seemed to open into thin air letting the beauty of the ranch inside. One wall, composed entirely of tinted glass, gave the room's occupants an unobstructed view of the frozen grassland and the splendor of the snowcapped mountains beyond. Even though everything was barren now, Mary knew in just a few short months the surrounding mountains would be lush and green, abundant with life. Her resolve firmed to convince the man to take a chance on her. Fiddler Creek was home. A home she didn't want to give up.

She admired the sanded pine floor covered here and there with colorful braided rugs. A huge stone fireplace dominated another wall. Two chocolate colored leather couches flanked it and a soft bearskin rug lay in front. It was the ideal picture of home and hearth.

Staring dreamily into space, she imagined a beautifully decorated blue spruce at Christmas with presents piled knee deep beneath it. She envisioned a loving couple nestled together watching with amused indulgence as black haired boys and delicate, angelic featured girls ripped open their brightly wrapped packages to see what Santa had brought them.

She refused to speculate on the reason why the couple bore a striking resemblance to herself and the man quickly disappearing down the hall.

"Get a move on," Luke yelled, his voice rudely interrupting her daydream. She snorted indelicately and muttered words of ire under her breath. She prayed he was not always so abrupt.

Following the sound of his voice, she silently encouraged herself to see this through to the end. She may have walked into the lion's den, but she had no intention of being on this evening's menu.

Lost in her thoughts, Luke realized Mary didn't see him stop at the entrance to the kitchen. His hands went out, stopping her forward motion as she plowed into him.

"I am so sorry," she apologized. Her hand flexed against the hard plane of his chest. The other had a death grip on her briefcase. "I wasn't watching where I was going."

Luke grunted in response and removed his hands. He could feel the heavy fullness of her breasts through the thick layer of her coat. Damn, but she was all woman. "No harm done. I'll introduce you to my grandfather later. Since the accident, he usually takes a nap this time of day. I wake him right before dinner."

"What accident?"

"He and my stallion, Lucifer, had a little disagreement. Grandpa broke his arm. That's why we need a nurse." Luke watched with narrowed eyes as she placed her briefcase on the counter and removed her parka. The dark blue garment had effectively hidden the color of her hair and her ample figure from his sight, but he'd known instantly who she was. He'd seen her occasionally with the Talbots and on his ranch last summer at the camp for delinquent kids. He indicated she should hang her parka by the door.

She walked across the floor to hang her coat on one of the hooks, the movement of her hips as fluid and graceful as any runway model. Luke could tell Mary appreciated her own body. It showed in the way she carried herself. And damned if he didn't appreciate her as well. Even though a little on the heavy side, her curves suited Luke just fine. It sickened him to look at women on television and in magazines who appeared little more than flesh over bones. To maintain their appearance he knew they survived on nothing more substantial than carrot sticks and water. Hadn't Debbie?

Hellfire, he cursed silently. Why had thoughts of his ex-wife haunted him so much today? The woman had been five foot of nothing. No meat to sustain her waif-like figure and no substance on the inside either.

He took a well-worn apron from its hook by the sink and forced his thoughts back to preparing dinner. A lot of men would feel awkward or silly performing such a feminine task, but not Luke. Thanks to his grandmother, he was as at home in the kitchen as he was rounding up cattle.

"How serious was your grandfather's injury?" Mary took a seat on the barstool, the movement causing her full, silvery blonde hair to sway.

Luke turned away, ignoring the enticing citrus scent emanating from his guest. An unexpected flare of awareness blossomed in his loins but he firmly squelched it. He had learned his lesson well with his ex-wife and he didn't need any remedial training. Luke Tanner and women didn't mix, plain and simple. This woman appeared to be no different. She was here because she needed something. Another demanding female he could do without.

Not for the first time, he wondered if being such a success was worth it. He had to believe his great-grandfather had found more happiness in his two-room shack than Luke did in the five-bedroom house that stood in its place. At least his ancestor had had a wife and family to keep him company. That first Tanner had known his family loved him for himself, not because his bank account had more zeros then the Circle T had cattle.

He peeled and chopped potatoes, welding the long, sharp knife with the ease and finesse of a sous chef. If he used a little more force than was absolutely necessary, he didn't admit it to himself.

"According to Doc Logan, Grandfather's break is a simple fracture and will heal just fine. But he did suggest we get someone to help out around here for a while. Grandpa is no longer able to cook and clean and I don't have time to play housekeeper."

"And I suppose I do, Mr. Tanner?" A blonde eyebrow quirked in inquiry.

"Doing a few dishes and cooking a few meals above your calling, Ms. Carter?" Luke watched as the beautiful face before him took on an outraged expression and her whole body quivered with an effort not to explode. It had been a long time since someone besides his grandfather had stood up to him.

The woman had spunk; he had to give her that. Maybe she was just what the doctor ordered to lift his grandfather out of the blue funk he'd fallen into lately. If the truth be told, they could use more than a little help. Even before the accident, he'd been thinking of getting someone in more frequently to clean. Eyeing the intriguing woman before him, he thought this might prove to be an interesting arrangement. A very interesting arrangement indeed.

As the silence stretched, he watched her become even more flustered. She parted her full lips and a small pink tongue came out to wet them, sending that same long forgotten shiver of awareness down his spine. He could tell she wanted nothing more than to march out the front door and to tell him to take his job offer and shove it where the sun didn't shine. She held her temper. Just barely.

"Would you like for me to cook dinner tonight?" She sounded as if she'd rather run naked through a cactus patch and he grinned to himself as she clenched her fists against the granite countertop.

"No, thanks, I've got everything under control," he answered. He finished the potatoes and put them on to boil. Pulling the makings for a salad from the fridge, he gestured toward the living room. "Why don't you go wait in there?"

"Yes, sir, anything you say sir," Mary mumbled under her breath as the arrogant man waved her away. Taking deep, calming breaths, she made her way into the spacious room that had captured her fancy just moments before.

She picked up a faded black and white photograph from the mantel. A man and woman stood, arms entwined, looking not at the camera but at each other with so much emotion it made Mary's chest ache. The man was tall and rugged and the woman, Mary noted with great satisfaction, had a well-rounded figure. She sighed, thinking she had been born in the wrong century. Apparently, the early mountain men of Wyoming liked their women with a little meat on their bones. As she studied the two blurred images, soft footsteps sounded behind her.

In walked a man who bore an uncanny resemblance to the one in the picture. All three of the Tanner men looked strikingly similar. Joseph Tanner was the handsomest of the three, Luke apparently having taken after his great-grandfather with his rawboned look. Joseph still cut a striking figure for a man in his seventies. Specks of white sprinkled his once jet-black hair and the proud set of his shoulders barely drooped.

Before she could introduce herself, he spoke. "That's a picture of my mother and father, Adam and Rachel Tanner. She had hair the color of copper and he stood as high as the mountains."

The reverent tone of his voice reflected the obvious love and pride he felt for his parents. Taking the picture from her hands, he studied it briefly before gently replacing it on the mantel. "She came here as a mail order bride and some say before that she worked in a brothel in St. Louis. But that didn't bother my dad. He said he loved her from the day she stepped off the train."

"We all have a past," Mary said, wanting to assure the elder gentleman that she had nothing against him because of his heritage. Having endured so much herself, she tried never to stand in judgment of anyone else.

"So we do, so we do." The man agreed. He gave her a measuring look. "But sometimes that past interferes with the present and the future."

Mary saw the look he threw her and returned it in full. She had been tested many times by her elderly patients. Their generation judged a person on self-worth and not material possessions. But the look in Joseph's eyes seemed to reflect something else entirely. A warning perhaps?

"Dinner's ready." Luke's voice boomed from the kitchen, startling her.

"Is he always so curt?" she asked irritably.

Joseph chuckled and placed his hand on her elbow to guide her from the room. "He's always been an impatient sort. Even as a child. Seemed to learn to ride before he could walk. Drove my Emma crazy."

They arrived at the table in time to see Luke placing large pieces of steak on a platter. Bowls of creamy mashed potatoes, fresh green beans, and the garden salad Mary had watched him fix sat on the end of the serving bar. Without a word, they each helped themselves to the delicious smelling side dishes.

"This tastes heavenly, but I wish you had allowed me to help." She still smarted over his comment about menial labor being beneath her. He had a lot to learn about the nursing profession if he thought hard physical labor didn't play a part.

She cut into her steak gingerly. Looking up, she caught Luke's eye and smiled sheepishly. She hated meat that wasn't well done. "This is perfect. Thank you."

"Most women like their steak burnt to a crisp."

Mary's eyes narrowed. "I'm not most women. And I don't care for people who label others. But you are correct; I don't like my meat to moo when I try to eat it." She gestured to his almost raw piece of steak, the smile that curved her lips sugary sweet, if not downright condescending.

Joseph laughed at Luke's steely expression, making Mary realize that very few people ever talked back to the man. She stabbed a green bean with a vengeance. Well, Mr. Tanner, she thought savagely, don't look now, but I'm about to rock your world.

After she took a few more bites, she turned her attention to Joseph, deciding to ignore the big man by her side. With the looks he kept casting her way, she'd be lucky if she didn't get indigestion. "Exactly what kind of ranch is this, Joseph?"

Luke answered before his grandfather could speak. "What kind of ranch do you think it is, city girl?" His disdain for her laced his voice. "An ostrich ranch?"

Mary threw him a frosty glare, determined not to let him intimidate her. "For all I know it might very well be. I believe they do quite well in Australia."

Luke muttered a colorful word under his breath, earning himself a warning glare from his grandfather.

"We raise cattle," Joseph said. "And Luke also has a fine string of purebred stallions. His stud service is quite impressive."

Mary sputtered and almost choked on her tea as not-so-innocent images of Luke flashed through her mind. Setting her glass on the table, she hoped neither man noticed the slight flush on her face. She breathed a sigh of relief as Joseph rose to refill his plate without saying a word.

"Well, well, well." Luke's voice whispered in her ear as he leaned across the space between them. Those enticing eyes bored into hers, as if he could look inside her very soul and discover all her hidden secrets and fantasies. "What naughty thoughts we're having Ms. Carter. Care to share?"

"Only in your dreams, buster," she shot back, mortified. If only he knew.

"You'd be surprised what dreams I have," he said softly, sitting back in his chair. His eyes turned a bright shade of green and held hers for endless moments. Joseph returned to the table and Luke turned his attention back to his meal.

Mary trembled. She could have sworn she'd seen a small spark of desire in his eyes. Then just like water on a flickering flame, the light had been extinguished and his face had taken on the hard, cynical expression she had become accustomed to in so short a time.

But then she knew she had only imagined that brief awareness. After all, who would want Mary Carter?

Pasting a smile on her face she turned back to Joseph. "How long have you been in the cast?"

"Only two weeks," he grumbled. "Doc said it would be another month or so before he would even consider taking it off."

"That's not very long. The time will go by before you know it." Mary consoled the older man with stories of other patients she had nursed with broken bones, delighting him with some hilarious antics.

Eventually she ran out of tales and grew silent. Laying her fork beside her plate, she waited while the two men finished up. She had decided over dinner not to proceed with her plan to ask Luke for the loan. She would think of something else. Something that had nothing to do with the rich rancher.

Once the men were done, she gathered up the dirty dishes and ran some warm water in the sink. She pushed up the sleeves of her sweater, determined to do the cleanup.

"Well, just don't stand there, Luke, help the girl." Behind her she heard Joseph scold his grandson and could just imagine the scowl the younger man sent his way. Hushed whispers floated back to her and she didn't have to guess at the content of their conversation. Luke's grandfather had not been very pleased with his grandson's behavior at the dinner table and she smiled at the thought of the large, formidable man being dressed down by his elder.

Several long minutes passed before she heard the scrape of a chair being pushed back. Seconds later a pile of dishes appeared at her elbow.

"This isn't necessary." Luke stood at her side, watching her with those dark green eyes.

"I know, but I want to help." Mary kept her head down, her eyes focused on the suds forming in the sink.

"Why? Do you think it will earn you brownie points? Make me grab my checkbook and give you the money on the spot?"

Let him think what he wanted. "You'll be happy to know I've changed my mind, Mr. Tanner. I'll find the money another way. Doing the dishes is simply my way of repaying you for your hospitality and dinner."

"Why?"

"Why what?" Mary rinsed a plate beneath a steady stream of cold water and tried to cool her rising temper at the same time. What an insufferable man! "Why wash the dishes? Because my mother did instill some manners in me. Believe me, it's only common courtesy, not a foolproof way to your wallet."

"You're damn right it's not. It would take more than a few household chores for that." His gaze traveled up and down her well-endowed figure, lingering on the rise and fall of her breasts beneath her sweater. Seeing the direction of his gaze, Mary's breathe quickened. His look made her think of the many delightful ways she could repay the big man.

She dropped the dish into the drainer and faced him. "What would it take, Mr. Tanner?" she asked her voice a husky dare. She knew this false bravado came from the hot edge of her temper, but she didn't care.

At her words his face closed up tighter than a pickle barrel. "More than what you have to offer, that's for sure."

Her face flooded with color at his insult. "Why you–"

"Did you two get the details all ironed out?" Joseph walked into the room, cutting off the searing retort Mary had been about to deliver.

She took a deep breath and turned toward Joseph, unmindful of the fact that Luke's gaze was again riveted to the front of her sweater.

Joseph did notice and tried to cover his chuckle with a cough. "When can you start?"

Mary gained control and looked at the other man. "I'm afraid I won't be able to stay, Joseph. I know I would have had a wonderful time looking after you, but I just can't."

"I'll give you the loan if you work for me." Luke's words, short and clipped, fell from tightened lips.

Mary looked from one man to the other, her mind torn between accepting the offer and proving the rancher wrong, and wanting to walk out the front door, never to look back.

Joseph took her arm and ushered her from the room. He threw his grandson one last hard look.

"It's simple, Mary. I need a nurse for a month, maybe longer. You need a loan. Once you leave, Luke will give you the loan and your business will be on top in no time. You'll also receive a salary while you're here. That should tide you over in the meantime."

"But he hasn't heard my proposal," she protested weakly, feeling as steamrolled as fresh laid asphalt but unable to think of a single protest.

Joseph waved aside her concerns. Within minutes, the older man had Mary bundled into her coat and seated in the borrowed truck. "Working here on the ranch will tell Luke all he needs to know. Be here bright and early tomorrow–well, not too early." He grinned and Mary returned the smile. He really was a sweet old man.

CHAPTER TWO

The crisp cold air of the early morning held the fragrant scent of the evergreens growing along the long, lonely stretch of road. The world was covered in a heavy frost as yet undisturbed by man or beast. But the beauty of the majestic scenery failed to soothe Luke's ragged nerves as he drove to his friend's house.

After tossing and turning for hours, he'd given up any hope of a full night's rest. At dawn's first light, he'd risen and dressed. His sleep–what little he'd gotten–had been filled with images of a silver haired nymph being chased by a thundering herd of cattle. He had no doubt yesterday's visitor had inspired his restlessness and the bizarre dreams.

He left the ranch with the sole intention of giving the good-hearted reverend a piece of his mind. Constantly yammering about how Luke should forget Debbie and get on with his life, he had no doubt who had inspired Mary's sudden interest in acquiring a loan. But Luke wasn't ready to start a relationship again. Not yet. Maybe never. The words of his ex-wife still haunted him in the dark hours of the night.

He pulled up in front of the small frame house and jumped from the truck. He knocked on the kitchen door, waiting with barely controlled patience for someone to answer. As soon as the door swung open, he began his tirade.

"What the hell do you mean, sending that woman out to my house?" he demanded. In his agitation, he paced back and forth in front of his bleary-eyed friend.

"Hell, Mark," he continued to curse, at a loss for the right words to explain the real reason why he didn't want Mary in his house. How did you tell a preacher that a complete stranger had stirred you to life, turned you inside out, and broken through a wall you believed to be impenetrable?

Luke took a crumpled pack of cigarettes from his coat pocket and pulled one out with his teeth. He lit it quickly. The raw burning sensation that followed almost made him choke. He hadn't smoked in years, but last night the uncontrollable craving had struck him and he'd knocked on the bunkhouse door, rousing a sleepy hand to bum a smoke. He slowly exhaled, watching the white smoke dissipate in the frosty air.

"See what that woman has made me do?" he grumbled, shaking the long, thin cylinder at his friend.

Mark held up one hand to stop his words. "Hold on a minute, Luke. Let me wake up. You're not making any sense. Back up and tell me what happened."

Luke drew in a ragged breath. He explained how his grandfather had hired Mary as his nurse for the next month or so in exchange for Luke giving her a loan when she left. His head of steam came to an abrupt end, and he stopped talking.

Mark nodded in approval. "That seems like a reasonable arrangement. I'm glad you decided to help."

Luke snorted in disgust. "I didn't." He started pacing again. "That's the problem."

"What's got you so worried, pal? Mary's a good nurse. She helped Jennifer after Jessica's birth. We couldn't have made it without her. And investing in her business also sounds like a wise move. Heck, if I had the extra money, I'd give it to her myself."

His words didn't impress Luke in the slightest. "You'd give money to the devil himself if he seemed pathetic enough."

"If it makes you feel any better, Jennifer tried to talk her out of it, but she wouldn't listen." Mark shrugged his shoulders as if to say he had done all that he could do.

Luke took another long drag of his cigarette. "So, this isn't another of your do-gooder schemes? You have no ulterior motive for sending Mary to the Circle T?"

"I'm hurt, Luke. I'm truly hurt that you could think that of me. This had nothing to do with me. You and your grandfather hired Mary. I didn't even suggest it, although I wish I had. Is Mary being there going to bother you?"

"Of course not." Luke realized he'd made his denial too quickly when he saw the gleam that entered his friend's eyes. "I've sworn off women, Mark, remember? I don't want a repeat of what happened with Debbie."

He'd never told anyone, not even his friend, what had transpired on his wedding night. How he'd been unable to maintain his desire long enough to consummate his marriage. Once she'd gotten the gold band on her finger, her true colors had come out with a vengeance. Luke had realized he'd made a mistake before they'd reached the hotel's honeymoon suite, but he'd married the woman and he'd been willing to stand by his decision.

Debbie had laughed while she ridiculed him. She'd gloated about how she'd fooled him by pretending to want him just so she could get his money. She had hurled other taunts and insults about his looks and his masculinity as she left the five-star room. Her words had cut to the quick and it had taken him a long time to get over the pain.

He realized now that his failure in the marital bed had been a direct result of his lack of love for his wife. He'd used Debbie as much as she'd used him. He'd been looking for someone to love; she'd been looking for an easy meal ticket. Neither had gotten their heart's desire.

So now if he found himself yearning for something more, for someone to believe in him, yes, someone to love, he squelched those feelings and worked even harder on his ranch.

As if sensing his inner turmoil, Mark broke into his thoughts impatiently. "How you can let that woman still get to you is beyond me."

"Your job is to forgive."

"My job is not to pass judgment," Mark corrected. "Which I don't. But the woman wanted your money and your ranch, Luke. And she went about it any way that she could. What she did had nothing to do with true love between a man and a woman."

Luke finished his cigarette and tossed the butt aside. He watched as it made a wide arch before landing on the frozen ground, the glowing end extinguished by the melting frost. He didn't acknowledge his friend's support, he didn't have to. Even though he rarely said the words aloud, Mark knew the high esteem with which Luke regarded him.

"I just hope I don't regret this." He turned to leave.

"You won't," Mark grinned and slapped him on the back. "I promise."

"Yeah, just like you promised that horse I bought off old man Winchester was saddle broken."

"Hey, you can't blame me for that," he protested. "He just didn't like your looks.

"I have to admit I had a damn fine time showing him who was boss." Finally, Luke grinned, his bad mood lifting after speaking to his friend.

After saying goodbye, he strode from the porch, waving one last time as he pulled from the graveled drive and headed out of town. Last night he'd decided to let his grandfather welcome Mary to the

Circle T. He would attend the monthly cattle auction in Newport and leave the two to settle in.

He'd taken one look at the curvy woman and felt his hard won control start to slip. A little time away was needed to shore up his defenses.

"Damnation." He slapped his hand against the steering wheel. He'd be better off just keeping his distance. And this trip was the perfect beginning. Maybe this attraction to Mary was the end of his long dry spell with women. A cowboy with a pocket full of change could always find himself a good time no matter how ugly he happened to be.

Several days later Mary woke slowly then sat up with a start.

"Pooh bear," she muttered. The time on the bedside clock read half past nine. Well past the time she should have been up and about.

A chill permeated the early morning air even though the calendar proclaimed it to be mid-May. She bounded from bed. Time to decide what to wear. Joseph had been most adamant about her not wearing a uniform, but clothes had been her enemy for a long time. For years, the only fashion available for women of Mary's size were shapeless garments made of polyester. Within the last few years, designers had finally wised-up and started producing clothes for the plus-sized woman made of silk and satin and in beautiful flowing lines that flattered rather than fattened. But Mary didn't have anyone in her life to care whether she wore the newer, sexier garments or not.

She decided on a blue jogging suit. The fit wasn't too bad and she had to admit the color made a perfect foil for her silvery hair. Catching her reflection in the mirror, she stuck out our tongue and her image grinned back. Yes, she was what some would consider pretty, but she knew not many men looked past her generous curves. Which saddened and upset her.

Above anything else, she wanted to be a wife and mother. She believed with all her heart that somewhere out there, there existed a man who would love her, respect her, and cherish her until her dying day. A man who could fill the deep, aching void she felt inside. She just hadn't met him yet. With her luck, she thought grumpily, remembering the picture of Luke's great-grandparents, he'd probably been born in the 1800's and she lived in the 21st century.

She tucked away her sad thoughts and made her way down the back stairs to the kitchen. She'd arrived at the Circle T packed for a month's stay eager to spar with the burly rancher, only to find that Luke had left town. Joseph had welcomed her with open arms and Mary pushed aside the deep sense of disappointment.

She poured herself a cup of steamy coffee and hoped the jolt of caffeine would pry her heavy eyelids apart. Her dreams over the past few nights had been filled with a green-eyed cowboy she'd just as soon forget.

"Good morning, Mary."

Luke's deep voice sent shivers up and down her spine. From her first meeting, his captivating voice had become one of her greatest weaknesses. He could probably talk about branding cattle and turn her insides to mush.

"Good morning, Mr. Tanner." She willed herself to sound and look casual as she turned to face him.

A red checked shirt topped a pair of faded jeans. To her, he looked as sexy as John Wayne ever did on the big screen. Mary tried to calm her erratic pulse as she took a seat at the scarred wooden table.

"I see you've already had breakfast." She waved a hand at the neatly washed and stacked dishes.

"Yep," Luke replied, his expression unreadable. "I figured since I hadn't had the dubious honor of eating anything you had prepared, I'd better have at least one good meal today."

Luke's mouth curved into a grin that transformed his rough features into a thing of beauty but his words still ignited Mary's as usual too-quick temper. "Now listen here, Mr. Tanner..."

"Simmer down, sweetheart. I was only having a bit of fun. My grandfather told me you're a great cook." He walked to the sink and dumped his coffee before picking up his faded Stetson.

"Well, your 'bit of fun' was at my expense and I don't like it," she snapped. He'd been gone for four days and she'd been looking forward to seeing him again.

"The name's Luke." He placed the hat on his head then bent down to whisper in her ear. "I can't say I care much for jogging, but this suit is a blessing to any man's morning."

Whistling he opened the back door and let it slam close behind him.

Mary felt the blood rush to her cheeks at his flattery. She took a sip of her coffee and wondered if she had imagined the feel of his lips on her ear. It didn't matter. She could still feel the warmth of his breath and hear the deep timber of his sexy voice. That would definitely fuel a few more of her impossible dreams.

Ten minutes later Joseph's arrival forced her from her musings. She realized she hadn't even started breakfast and hastened to put water on to boil for their morning bowl of oatmeal. Joseph placed two slices of bread in the toaster before taking a seat at the table.

"Boy am I starving this morning." The older man grinned. "It must be all that fresh air we've been getting." On the second day at the ranch, Mary had suggested some light exercise, nothing too strenuous, just short walks around the ranch yard. Since his arm was broken, Joseph hadn't been doing his daily chores or getting the exercise he was used to.

"This won't take but a minute." She waved to the boiling pot. "I guess I slept in late this morning, too." On chilly mornings when his arthritis bothered him, Joseph didn't raise much before nine. She pulled a knife from the drawer to butter the toast then realized she already had one. Determined to get her mind back on track, she finished the toast and placed a bowl of creamy cereal on the table.

"How are you this bright and beautiful morning, my dear?" Joseph opened the sugar bowl and put two heaping tablespoons on his cereal. Mary hid a smile. She'd replaced the pure cane sugar with a substitute and he had yet to comment on the difference.

"I want to talk to you. I called Dr. McAllister yesterday and got an update on your condition." She spooned the sugar substitute into her second cup of coffee.

"Now, now, Mary, why bother Doc Logan? I'm doing fine. I hope you're not getting bored way out here in the back of beyond." It took the better part of an hour to drive into town from the ranch and, with no transportation; Mary hadn't left the Circle T since she'd arrived.

"Of course not. I'm used to entertaining myself. And don't try to change the subject," she admonished with a smile. "The doctor seemed more concerned with your general health than he did your fall. Apparently your blood pressure is up and so is your blood sugar."

"Nonsense," Joseph blustered. "I'm fit as a fiddle."

"If you're so fit, then why do you need me here?" She knew he could have serious problems if he didn't take some remedial action now.

"Now don't be thinking I don't need you, Mary. I really do. You can show me what I can and can't eat and make sure I take my medications on time. My cast should be ready to come off in a few more weeks. You might even need to help me with my therapy afterwards. Say you'll stay until then. Please?" He looked at her pitifully.

"Alright. But I want to do something else besides being at your beck and call and doing a little cooking." Still smarting over Luke's challenge of doing housework, she continued. "Luke said you were taking care of the house before the fall. Didn't you have a cleaning lady?" Mary hated to admit to the curiosity burning inside about the other people in Luke's life. Especially if there just happened to be a woman somewhere in the mix.

The old man shook his head. "It's just us, bachelor number one and bachelor number two. As you can see, we tend to neglect this old house. You should have seen it in my mother's day and before my Emma passed away. The floors shone and the windows sparkled." Joseph's eyes took on a faraway expression.

"I can't promise to be Ms. Suzy Homemaker," Mary cautioned, her heart aching in sympathy for the older man's loss, "but I can wield a mean broom and mop when I take a notion."

Joseph rose and placed his dirty dishes in the big stainless steel sink. "That would be fine, Mary. But we didn't hire you to be a scullery maid. Tell me what you want to do and I'll get one of the ranch hand's wives to help you with the heavy stuff like I did for Emma. In the meantime, I'll give you the nickel tour."

Even though she'd been dying of curiosity, Mary had so far confined herself to her bedroom and the general living areas. Joseph and Mary usually retired at the same time each night. She hadn't wanted to be intrusive and spent the early evening hours in her room, restless and lonely. She now knew the bed creaked, dust bunnies multiplied in the corner, and the faucet in the connecting bathroom leaked.

"Don't you mean the ten cent tour?"

"Nah, things are a lot cheaper out here, honey." They both laughed at his corny joke as he allowed her to precede him from the room.

The first door on the right at the top of the stairs housed the master bedroom. Luke's room. Mary entered it slowly. This room, hidden behind its solid oak door, held the deepest fascination for her. She sighed as she scanned the spacious room, hoping to catch a more revealing glimpse of the man she now called boss. But no photographs or personal items cluttered the surfaces. As if reading her thoughts, Joseph spoke.

"Emma and I had many good years in this room but the memories were just too strong for me. I finally convinced Luke to move in here about a year ago. He hasn't done much with it I'm afraid to say."

Mary straightened the covers on the king-sized bed. "You mean he didn't use this room during his marriage?"

"No," Joseph shook his head. "He didn't feel right usurping me. And quite frankly, I didn't like the girl so I didn't push the issue. If they had stayed together, I would have gladly moved to another room."

Mary felt her heart pound. She didn't want to hear all the intimate details of Luke's marriage. And yet she did. Did a failed marriage lie at the root of his black moods?

After helping her straighten the bed, Joseph motioned for her to open the door at the other side of the room. Mary walked in and lost her heart. Love seeped from all four corners of the surprisingly large space. The walls, painted a pale yellow, provided the perfect contrast for a large mural of snow-white bunnies frolicking in an enchanted forest. A thick layer of dust covered the crib, rocker, and changing table, but the beauty of the antique furniture had not dimmed with time.

"This room hasn't been used since Luke was a baby," Joseph said, a look of sadness in his eyes. "Emma saved all of his things. They're stored in the attic but I don't think my grandson will ever have any use for them. I've told him I'd like to see a great-grandchild or two before I go, but the most important thing to Luke right now is the Circle T. The Tanner land." Joseph sighed and Mary could sense something troubled her patient.

"Is that wrong?" she questioned. "I would think you'd be glad Luke showed such an interest in running the ranch."

"Oh, I am," Joseph hastened to reassure her. "It's just that he hasn't found the true spirit of the land yet."

Mary couldn't help but ask. "The true spirit?"

Joseph looked her straight in the eye, the faded green reminding her so much of Luke's. "It all means nothing–the land, the wealth, the success– unless you have someone to share it with."

"I'm sure Luke will get married again when the time is right."

Mary's heart beat a frantic tattoo against her ribs at the thought of Luke marrying. At the thought of Luke marrying her.

That brought her up short. When had her feelings changed from a slight crush to a full-blown obsession? When you saw just how sexy and appealing he was up close and personal the little voice inside her taunted.

For her own sanity she decided to change the subject. "Where are Luke's parents now? Does he have any brothers and sisters who could use these lovely things?" Her fingers caressed the smooth surface of the dresser.

"Luke is an only child. His parents didn't have the most ideal marriage. They married too young. By the time he turned eighteen my son, Wayne, had decided he didn't want to be a rancher and headed off to college where he met Luke's mother, Madeline. They were the perfect pair, both selfish to the bone. Ten months later they had Luke. Six months after that, Wayne knocked on our door saying they couldn't handle raising a child. Emma and I filed for custody and brought Luke up as our own." Joseph shook his head sadly, lost in his memories.

"Where are Luke's parents now?" No one, not even the most die-hard gossips in town, had ever mentioned the missing Tanners.

Joseph fingered the warm wood of the cradle. "They're both dead. They died in a car crash soon after Luke turned three. They had moved to the city and were living the high life on the trust fund I'd set up for Wayne when he was a child."

Mary didn't know what to say and Joseph had apparently decided he'd said enough. "Come on. I'll show you the rest of the house."

CHAPTER THREE

Luke rode hard and fast to the south pasture trying to make up for lost time. He should have been out on the range an hour ago. With a muttered expletive, he jammed his hat down tight as the wind threatened to tear it off.

What had possessed him to touch her? Just five minutes in Mary's presence and he couldn't keep his hands off her. Who was he trying to kid? Just waiting for her to come downstairs had made anticipation build like a child on Christmas morning.

He'd thought the slow, sensual heat he'd felt when she'd first appeared on his front doorstep had been a fluke, but apparently it had merely disguised a raging brushfire. When he touched her, his whole body responded.

Heaven knew he hadn't felt any type of sexual desire for a woman in more than two years. Not even with the young and forward groupies who followed the rodeo circuit and hung out at the stockyard sales. Like the ones in Newport who had made it perfectly clear they would be willing to help him pass the dark lonely nights. He hadn't joined up with any of the women, though. Instead he'd spent his free time holed up in his hotel room, watching re-runs of Gunsmoke and thinking of Mary. Something he had to stop doing. And soon.

He reined Lucifer in and let his eyes take in his surroundings. He'd spent the whole of his thirty-eight years making the Circle T the most successful cattle operation around, building upon what his great-grandfather and grandfather had started. A few lucky breaks and some shrewd investments on Wall Street had ensured the future of the ranch well into the next millennium.

Tanner land. Land passed down from generation to generation. The land was his life. The land never left you, never betrayed you. It was the one constant, never changing fact of life a man could depend on. Something even the most cynical and barren of heart could believe in. It gave you everything and asked nothing in return.

"Hello, boss." His foreman, a grizzled old cowhand, greeted him as he swung gracefully from his horse.

The closed expression on Luke's face did not daunt the older man. He had been foreman on the Circle T for too many years. First for Joseph and now Luke. Very little escaped the tall, silent man.

"Good morning, Hawk. Anything new I should be aware of?"

"We've got some cattle lost in the lower pastures according to the new guy, Johnson. I thought I'd send a couple of men out to round them up while we finish up here.

Luke knelt near a bundle of posts that needed to be separated. The hands spent the cold winter days repairing the broken down fences in preparation for the spring roundup that was almost upon them. "How are the new guys doing?"

"Okay, I guess." Hawk's bronze features twisted into a frown." One of 'em comes with good recommendations from the Bar M. He's a good family man who's had a run of bad luck. But the other guy, Johnson, I'm not so sure about. Some of the men have complained that he has a loud mouth and a mean temper."

Luke immediately thought of another sassy individual who had invaded his life but quickly pulled his wayward thoughts from Mary and concentrated on his foreman's report.

"We're short-handed so I guess we can't be too choosy," Hawk continued. "Dang it, I wish those other fellers hadn't quit." He slapped his sweat stained hat against his thigh, the large gray Stetson showing other marks of his frequent abuse.

Luke shrugged. "It happens, Hawk. The bright lights, the big city. It's hard to keep the men entertained way out here." He freed the posts with one final clip of the wire cutters and rose to his feet. He kept his voice low as he warned his foreman. "Keep an eye on the guy though. I don't want any surprises. And I'll see about the strays."

He hoisted himself back into the saddle and rode in the direction Hawk had mentioned. Rounding up strays was a tiresome, time-consuming job; one he usually didn't volunteer for. But today he had a lot of serious thinking to do. For the first time in over two years, he felt like a man again. A man with needs and desires. Trouble was, he didn't know what to do about it.

Several hours later, Luke halted in mid-stride upon entering the kitchen. The room qualified as a disaster area. Cans and boxes of food littered every available surface and pots and pans overflowed from the open cabinet doors. But what stopped him in his tracks was the picture of Mary.

Even though no one, kind or otherwise, could call Mary a small woman, she was attractive. A generous woman, he could almost hear his grandfather say, with enough curves and valleys to keep a man warm through a cold Wyoming winter. And he definitely had no problem with Mary's size. He'd dated all types of women–tall women, short women, small women, large women. In the dark they were all the same, a warm body and a pair of arms to hold you until the morning light. Unfortunately, none of them could completely chase away the loneliness.

He stood for several more minutes, watching as she stretched to reach the top shelf of the high oak cabinets. As she worked, she sang along with the country western tune on the radio, her soft voice filled the room. Voluptuous hips swayed to the rhythm of the music, drawing Luke's eyes. The baggy sweats of that morning had been replaced with mid-thigh cotton shorts. A long, oversized t-shirt slipped from one shoulder to reveal a large expanse of creamy skin. A turquoise clip held her long flowing hair away from her face. She looked young and carefree, sexy enough to entice any man.

For just a moment his breathing increased and he forgot why he had returned to the house. A sharp stab of pain in his forearm quickly reminded him.

He must have made some small sound alerting her to his presence for suddenly she swung around. Immediately her eyes spied the blood soaked sleeve of his shirt and she flew to his side in a flash. "Oh, Luke," she exclaimed. "What happened?"

"What the hell does it look like? And just what do you think you're doing?" Luke demanded. With his good arm, he gestured at the mess around him.

"I'm cleaning the house. Part of our bargain if you remember correctly," she snapped back. "Now hold still and let me take a look at your arm."

Mary examined his wound, making soft purring noises in the back of her throat. It pulled at Luke's heart, this show of concern. It disturbed him, physically and mentally, that she could turn him inside out with just a touch.

He realized he'd poured himself into the ranch way too long and figured he needed to get back into the swing of things, start socializing, and find himself a woman who could fulfill his needs without any strings attached. When women found out just how much money stood behind the Tanner name it was easy, too easy, to establish a mutually satisfying relationship. But at the end of their time together, no hearts were broken, no dreams of white knights shattered. He had gotten what he wanted and needed. A couple of hours where the loneliness didn't eat away at his soul like a cancer. Only with his ex-wife had he allowed the hot flush of desire to evolve into something more. And look where that had gotten him.

"I can take care of it myself. First aid is a necessary fact of life on a ranch, Ms. Carter." He removed his arm from her soft touch. Infection presented a serious risk when you worked with animals and Luke insisted that even the slightest injury be taken seriously. Even his own. A rancher couldn't afford to be laid up for even one day.

It had given him an excuse to come back to the house. He could just as easily have had the bunkhouse cook, Rooster, patch him up. The man had done it many times before. Reluctantly Luke admitted to himself that he'd wanted to see Mary again. He enjoyed her quick wit, even the stinging insults she threw his way. But he also knew nothing could come of his fledgling feelings. Nothing.

Abruptly he stepped around her and headed to his bedroom. He could feel Mary watching him as he walked away and knew she would be worrying her bottom lip with her pearly white teeth in concern. She'd done it that first night on the ranch when she'd debated picking up her brief case and walking away. Why he noticed such things, he didn't understand. Yet he found himself wanting to soothe her tortured lips with his own.

He looked down at his blood soaked sleeve and realized he'd refused her help a little too quickly. It was going to hurt like the devil to remove his shirt. And even if his male pride allowed him to ask, after the brusque way he left, he doubted she'd be too willing to assist him now.

"Come into the bathroom." Mary burst through the door without knocking and Luke allowed himself a fleeting smile as he followed her into his bathroom. Apparently her compassionate heart had gotten the better of her temper.

As soon as he entered the room, he knew he'd made a grave error. He became aware of his size as he towered over her. She pulled his arm under a warm stream of water, forcing his hard frame against her soft curves and desire flowed through him like a molten river of lava. He groaned silently as his body instinctively responded to the feel of this woman.

"What happened? It looks like you had a fist fight with a briar thicket and lost."

"I did," Luke said through gritted teeth as she worked the fabric from the torn skin. "An ungrateful mamma threw me into a thorn bush when I tried to rescue her precious baby."

Mary looked up at him, grimacing in sympathy. "I know this must hurt. I'll try to be as gentle as possible."

To distract himself from the pain and the feel of her lush body, he released the barrette holding her hair, and ran the silken strands through his fingers. "You have beautiful hair," he murmured.

"As opposed to the rest of me?" she quipped. He heard her breath catch in the back of her throat as her hair caught on the pad of his work-roughened palm. It had been so long since he'd touched a woman. Felt the softness.

"That's not what I meant," he said. "And you know it."

"I do?" Her voice held a note of skepticism.

Luke narrowed his eyes. "Can't you take a damn compliment like a normal woman?"

Mary's shrug caused the blouse to slide further off her shoulder to reveal the satin strap of a peach colored bra. "Not many people, especially men, pay me compliments."

"Well, they should. You're a fine looking woman." His tone was solemn but he sensed she still didn't believe him. Before he could say more, she stepped back to inspect her handy work.

"There. I think that does it.

Luke removed his soiled shirt and immediately regretted the action as soon as he saw the bright red flush that stained Mary's cheeks. He hadn't meant to embarrass her.

"I'll soak that later." With jerky movements he threw the shirt in the claw-footed bathtub. He started to leave but she stopped him.

"Wait. I need to clean the cuts." He watched as she removed the first aid items from the medicine cabinet.

"This is going to sting," she cautioned, holding his arm over the sink once again. With a brief, sympathetic glance at his face, she poured antiseptic over the open cuts.

"Hell, woman! Are you trying to kill me?" He jerked his arm away, grabbing a clean towel from the shelf. Still swearing, he left the bathroom and took a seat on the edge of the bed. He removed the towel and took a good look at his injuries for the first time. Now cleaned, some of the cuts looked downright nasty and a few probably needed stitches.

"Give me those." He reached for the bandages Mary held in her hands. She'd followed him out, standing before him with a militant look in her gray eyes.

"I'm the nurse." She batted away his hands and knelt between his legs. "These probably need stitches, you know."

His frowned at her suggestion, even though he'd thought the same thing himself. Her tone made him feel like a scolded child.

"But then, you're as bad as your grandfather. It would take a two foot gore hole from a bull to get either of you to go to the doctor."

He smiled, watching her bent head. With very little effort, he could see her in this room, in his bed, in the dark of the night, the moonlight turning her hair the color of deep, pure silver. This time the desire he felt cut sharp and swift, like the blade of a knife. He placed the towel strategically over the front of his jeans.

With a determination borne of years of experience, he clamped down hard on such thoughts. "What has my grandfather been up to now?"

"His blood pressure is up. Dr. McAllister is concerned."

"What?" Luke growled. "Why didn't he tell me?"

8

Mary finished and rose to her feet. "He didn't want you to worry."

Luke strode across the room, away from the temptation of Mary. Retrieving a clean shirt from a chest of drawers, he fumbled to button it.

"Here, let me help." Her smaller hands moved his larger, clumsy ones aside.

"Is it serious?" He breathed in the clean, dewy scent of her skin.

"What?" She started as if she had been lost deep in thought. But he knew that couldn't be the case. Mary certainly wasn't standing in his room mooning over the likes of him. He was no woman's gift from God. Outside of his looks, which would never win him a beauty contest, he'd grown too rough, too set in his ways to cause a woman's heart to pound with desire. He knew his value to women and it came through his wallet, not his flesh.

"Grandpa. Is his blood pressure a problem?"

Mary shook her head. "Not right now. But it could be. I think he needs to see the doctor before his next scheduled checkup."

"Set up a time, and I'll take you." Against his will, he lifted his hand, following the flow of her hair across the crown of her head, the nape of her neck and down the curve of her spine. "You should wear it down more often. It suits you."

"Thank you." This time she smiled at his compliment and he allowed himself his own small grin. Apparently he'd gotten through her stubborn skin after all.

His finger traced the line of her jaw. "You're welcome. I'm fine now, Mary. Thanks for the help."

He pulled away and fastened his shirt. A man could only stand so much torment. And being next to Mary was the sweetest kind of torment known to man.

CHAPTER FOUR

"**S**he's a mighty fine figure of a woman, boss." Hawk pointed to Mary as she walked out of the bunkhouse kitchen almost a week later. Luke lifted his head from unsaddling Lucifer and gave the other man a quelling look. Hadn't he said pretty much the same words to Mary the day she'd bandaged his arm and received a taunted barb in return for his trouble? He wondered how she would react to his crusty foreman saying them now. Probably smile and give the old coot a kiss.

Of course his withering look didn't faze Hawk. The other man just smiled and continued to talk. "And it appears I'm not the only one around who thinks so."

Mary had stopped at the corral talking to the new man, Luther Johnson.

"What's Johnson doing here?" Luke demanded, his tone hard and flat. He tightened the cinch, uncomfortable with the stab of jealousy he felt.

Hawk's knowing gaze missed little as he answered. "All the hands are in the house pasture. We got a late start this morning, remember?"

"From now on keep the men away from the house. I don't pay them to socialize. I pay them to work." He walked out of the barn and headed for the corral. By the time he reached the couple, that stab of jealousy became a raw, open wound. "Get going, Johnson. The other men are ready to leave."

"So they are boss." The man straightened, insolence palpable in each movement of his body as he pushed back the brim of his hat. It took every ounce of Luke's iron control not to flatten the man where he stood. He stared at Mary like a thirsty man looking at a long, cool drink of water.

"See you later, honey." The cowboy smiled, revealing slightly crooked teeth as his gaze raked over Mary one last time.

Luke saw the shudder that shook Mary's frame as the man walked away and cursed. "What did he say to you?"

"Nothing much, just welcoming me to the ranch."

Luke couldn't let it go, a surge of fierce protectiveness rushing through him. He'd seen men like Johnson all his life, men who flirted with everything on two legs. He knew a pretty face and a few sweet words could turn any woman's head. Even Mary's. And he didn't like that thought. Not one bit.

"Are you sure? If any of the hands give you trouble, tell me or Hawk and they'll be dealt with."

"Okay," Mary smiled. "But I can handle the Johnsons of the world. By the way, I made an appointment for your grandfather with the doctor in the morning."

Luke nodded. "Fine, I'll take you to town myself. What time?"

"Ten o'clock."

"Good, I don't like the looks of this weather." Dark storm clouds gathered in the east, a sure sign of rain. "The forecasters are calling for the temperature to drop and, if we get any precipitation, I'm afraid it'll turn to freezing rain or even snow. That should give us time to see what's going to happen."

"Surely it doesn't snow in May?"

"Hell honey, I've seen it flurry in July. Believe me, I'm ready for spring." The long, harsh days of winter were filled with the tedious task of feeding cattle which left a man's mind free to think of ways to pass the equally long, lonely nights. And since Mary had come to live at the Circle T, Luke's mind had gone into overdrive, thinking of ways the two of them could spend the hours from dusk till dawn in the sweet, warm comfort of his bed.

"Well, I guess I'd better going."

He heard the hesitation in her words and it knocked at the fortress surrounding his own lonely heart. This was the first conversation they'd had in days. He'd avoided her ever since the day in his bedroom when she'd fixed his cuts, grunting his way through supper and earning himself silent reprimands from his grandfather.

Luke settled his hat further down on his head, but didn't move away either. All at once he felt a deep, driving need to ease a little of both their pain. What would it hurt to spend some time with Mary?

"What were you doing at the bunkhouse? Giving away more of my chocolate chip cookies?" Since discovering his sweet tooth, Mary made sure something was always around. He didn't want to think about how she could satisfy his other carvings.

She threw him a look that reminded him of his grandmother when she'd caught him raiding the cookie jar as a youngster. "Yes I did, but there's a batch cooling in the kitchen just for you, Mr. Tanner."

"Just wanted to make sure you knew who signed your paycheck." When her expression lost some of its shining luster, he cursed the slip of his tongue. The last thing he wanted was to remind her of their arrangement and why she was really here. "The boys appreciate your efforts, Mary. And so do I. Did your mother teach you how to cook?"

"No." Mary turned to face him. "My mother wouldn't know a chocolate chip from a peanut."

"So where did you learn?"

"Here and there. Every time dad got a new assignment, we got a new cook and housekeeper. One of the privileges of the rank and file. Most weren't adverse to teaching a pesky girl how to cook."

"So your dad's in the military?"

"Not anymore. He retired a couple of years ago and moved Mom to Florida."

"I bet you miss them." Luke studied her from beneath the brim of his hat.

"I do miss them. But not the moving."

"I guess you're not the traveling kind."

"No, I'm not." She watched as two cowboys led the horses out of the barn and into the corral. "All I've ever wanted was a small piece of land and a big view. It's hard not having a room of your own or even a swing set in the backyard. The way Daddy went from station to station, we didn't know from one year to the next where we would be or what kind of house we would have. I'm glad I didn't say no when Jennifer asked me to visit after she moved here. I love this place. She's an army brat, too, you know. That's how we met."

"Yeah, Mark mentioned that a time or two. If I recall, it took some convincing on his part before she agreed to move to Fiddler Creek." Luke refused to let the wistfulness of her tone get to him. Refused to think how it would be if he offered her a piece of his land, a piece of his soul, and all of his heart.

Just then Hawk came out, leading two pregnant mares. "Oh, would you look at them. They're so beautiful," Mary exclaimed as she stepped on the first rung of the fence. The move pushed her breasts high, giving him a perfect view of her body and making his hands itch to grasp the firm flesh hidden behind a long western style shirt.

"I wish I could ride."

"Have you ever ridden?" Luke moved closer. So close that his breath stirred the fine tendrils of hair at the nape of her neck and his lungs filled with her soft lemon scent. Despite his suggestion, she'd pulled her hair in a ponytail once again. She looked cute and sassy. And desirable. Damned desirable. Like a bolt of lightning he realized he wanted to make love to this woman.

Make love hell, Tanner, his libido shouted, you want to have sex. Hot, raw sex. And not just to prove you could. Making love required a commitment of emotion, something he shied away from giving. That brought him up short. Had his heart betrayed his body? Had he lost the ability to be a man through his unwillingness to admit to being human? To acknowledge the fact that he needed the warmth and closeness of someone other than himself?

"No," Mary answered, breaking into his thoughts. "I never learned to ride. My family never stayed in one place long enough to own a house, much less a horse."

"You should have gotten one of the boys to teach you last year at that camp," he said. He knew she'd been there but hadn't spoken to her. They few times he'd gone out to the site she'd been surrounded by children. And now that he gave it some thought, he realized that he had never seen Mary on a horse during the month and a half she'd been on the ranch.

The look she threw him spoke volumes.

"What?" he scowled darkly.

"I didn't want to find myself hanging at the end of a rope, strung up for being a horse thief," she replied tongue-in-cheek.

"Very funny," he said, his brows drawing together even more. "I did not say that."

"Whatever you say, Mr. Tanner. Whatever you say." Her smile lit up her face and Luke felt the kick all the way to his soul.

"Well, since you didn't take advantage of my kindness last summer, I'll give you a lesson now. If you want," he offered. He could picture Mary riding across the open range, her long hair whipping about her like a silver mane. The picture brought a rare smile to his rough features.

"Oh, Luke, would you really?" With a squeal of delight, she grabbed his hand and pulled him inside the barn.

Luke followed, savoring the unexpected feel of her hand in his. Once inside, he reluctantly let her go and headed to the nearest stall.

"This is Lady Jane." He rubbed the patch of white on the nose of a beautiful sorrel mare. "Come get acquainted."

"She's beautiful. Aren't you girl?" Mary cooed. The large wet nose nudged her hand and she laughed as she opened her hand to show the animal it was empty. "Not today. You had your treat yesterday."

"So you're the one who's been spoiling my prize ponies." Luke's voice held a teasing note as he handed her a chunk of carrot. He watched as she fed the mare her treat, feeling his gut tighten. She looked right at home in his barn. In his house. In his bed.

"Guilty as charged. Joseph and I give them a treat on the mornings we walk. But I really want to feed *him*. You're both always gone when we walk." She started toward the black stallion housed apart from the others.

Luke moved with surprising swiftness for a man his size to come between her and the horse. "Stay away from Lucifer," he ordered, all traces of teasing erased from his voice.

He had been out early, sleep eluding him yet again. He'd come back to the house for more fencing supplies. The great stallion snorted and pawed the hard packed earth beneath at the sound of his owner's sharp tone.

"Take it easy, boy." Luke soothed the anxious horse. He took the bridle in a firm grip and reached into his pocket. Withdrawing another large chunk of carrot, he hesitated before feeding the animal.

"Well, don't just stand there. He motioned her forward. Since you've already spoiled the others, you might as well learn how to feed him."

Mary eagerly held out her hand. "I thought you said to stay away from him?"

"Only when you're by yourself. And don't get smart with me, lady." He straightened out her fingers and placed the carrot in the flat of her palm. "Feed him like this. Otherwise you might end up missing a finger or two. Lucifer likes to bite."

He stroked the velvety muzzle as the horse picked the treat from her hand. "Did grandpa tell you about the accident?"

Mary shook her head, giggling as the horse's lips tickled her palm. Despite Luke's warning, Lucifer ate with surprising delicacy.

"He came out to feed this beast and got pinned against the stall. He'd fed him a hundred times before, but Lucifer is unpredictable at best." He looked her straight in the eye and said again, "Stay away from him unless I'm with you."

Their eyes held for long seconds until she nodded in agreement. "Which horse can I ride?"

Taking a blanket from the wall, Luke saddled the red sorrel. "We'll go with Lady Jane for now. If you're a very good girl, I might take you out on Lucifer someday."

"Oh, goody, goody. The master has spoken," she muttered under her breath.

"What?" Luke asked, having heard every word.

"Nothing," she said, smiling sweetly.

He threw her a knowing look and positioned the left stirrup. "Put one foot here and swing yourself over her back." He gave her a boost. His hand lingered a bit longer than necessary on the soft curve of her derriere.

"Maybe this wasn't such a good idea." Once seated, Mary clutched the saddle horn with both hands and he saw a small glimmer of fear appear in her gray eyes. He paid no attention to her protest and led the horse slowly from the barn.

"Relax, sweetheart. Feel the movement of the horse." He watched as she accustomed herself to Lady Jane's gait. They took several turns around the corral before Luke let out the rope, spurring Lady Jane into a faster rhythm.

Before long the rain, which had threatened all morning came with a vengeance. Luke reined in Lady Jane and helped Mary dismount. His fingers gripped her waist and her loose shirt bunched beneath his hands. He frowned as he realized she used her clothing as a shield to hide herself from the world. And from him. Instantly, he imagined her draped in something clingy and silky. Revealing.

"Come on." He pulled her into the dryness of the barn. Within minutes he had Lady Jane unsaddled, rubbed down and back in her stall. He leaned against the rail as he removed his hat. A quick shake of his head dispelled the drops of rain that had gathered. Outside, the rain fell in sheets, hitting the metal roof of the barn. The hay in the loft muffled the sound, cocooning them in a world all their own.

He watched for several minutes as she rubbed her arms against the chill in the air. Finally, he tugged her into the V of his splayed legs and moved her hands out of the way. His body tightened as he noted the contrast of the color of their skin and the compatibility of their sizes. He had always felt uncomfortable around Debbie and most of the other women he dated. As if at any moment he might break them in two if he held them too hard. He had never once allowed his passion to become uncontrollable for fear he would hurt them. With sudden insight, he knew those feelings had contributed to his performance–or lack thereof–on his wedding night.

But with Mary he could see himself completely losing control. His instincts told him she would be the perfect lover in so many ways.

"You're going to freeze to death," he muttered as he briskly rubbed his hands up and down her arms.

"Oh, why did it have to rain?" Mary's voice held a breathless quality which he hoped resulted more from his touch than the short ride.

"It's just as well," he answered, his own voice a husky drawl. "If you'd ridden for much longer, you'd have been too sore to move in the morning."

Instantly they both became aware of the double entendre and his fingers tightened on her waist.

"Don't look at me like that," he demanded.

"Like what?"

He stared at her until bright red color flooded her face, his eyebrow arched. "You don't know much about men, do you?" Luke muttered as he tugged at the clip that bound her hair, freeing it to his touch. The long, blonde strands fell in waves about her shoulders. He wanted to bury his face in the silky softness. Instead he trailed his fingers through it and relished the shudder that run through her frame. "I think I deserve a thank you for teaching you how to ride, don't you?"

"I don't think that would be such a good idea," she said, trying to draw away.

"That's the second time you've said that. Don't you know what you want?" Luke's big hand wrapped around the nape of her neck, holding her still as he lowered his head. His warm breath caressed her cheek. "I know what I want. I want you."

He wanted to kiss her. He wanted to take her satin soft mouth just as he had a thousand times in his dreams. He knew she'd taste as tart and tangy as the juice from sun sweetened cherries.

She gnawed on her lower lip.

"Don't do that," he commanded.

She looked at him, still worrying the tender flesh.

"God, Mary," he groaned. "A man can only take so much. I've got to taste you, baby. Open your mouth for me."

"I don't think I should."

"Don't think, honey, just feel."

She was feeling alright. Her lips parted with a moan and Luke began his sensuous assault in earnest, licking the fullness of her lips before covering her mouth with his. He deepened the kiss, feeling her body jerk at the intimate brush of his tongue against hers.

"Easy, baby," He soothed her much as he had Lucifer earlier. She reminded him of a high-strung filly. New and untried. Eager and excitable. He growled as heat exploded inside of him, starting at his heart and racing outward. Never had he felt like this before from a simple kiss. He stroked the tip of his tongue over her small, even, white teeth and the roof of her mouth, urging her to open more fully to his touch. He devoured her mouth when she complied with a soft groan.

His touch grew rough and Mary whimpered, the sound as soft and low as that of a newborn kitten. Even at the sound of her distress, he refused to break the intimate contact with her sweet lips. But he drew back to nibble gently at the sweet curve of her mouth. Several moments passed before he ended the kiss. When she would have moved out of his embrace, his arms closed hard around her refusing to let her go.

He could feel her body quivering and the surprising trembling in his own limbs. Not that his quaking could be seen with the naked eye. No, this rumble started somewhere deep inside his soul. He felt the layers of ice that surrounded his heartbreak away, replaced by light and warmth.

He smoothed the hair from her face, hooking the stray strands behind her ears." I'm sorry. I didn't mean to scare you. I forget what an innocent you are."

"I'm not an innocent," she protested

Nudging her chin up, he asked. "You're a virgin, aren't you?"

To know no man had ever touched her warm skin in the most private act known between a man and woman sent the blood surging throughout his body.

Green eyes met gray. She jerked free. "I have nothing to be ashamed of, Luke Tanner. There are hundreds, no thousands of thirty-two year old virgins around."

"Let's not get carried away, little girl," he grinned, drawing her close once again despite her token protest. "I'm glad, Mary. Really glad." He nuzzled the side of her neck, his teeth lightly nicking the slender column of her throat as he whispered against her skin." Do you know what the thought of your innocence does to me?"

She let her hands flatten against his chest, her fingers found the thick matt of hair edging from beneath his shirt. With one hand he reached up and pulled the snaps apart. He pressed her hand to his naked skin and shuddered as she explored the newly exposed territory. "That's it, sweetheart. Touch me."

He pressed another string of biting kisses along the curve of her jaw before turning his attention to the shell of her ear. He traced its delicate outer rim with his tongue. Fierce waves of desire washed over him as she rose to her tiptoes and shyly echoed his caress. He knew she would be just as eager to learn how to please him in other ways. The thought fanned the fire already burning in his belly.

He pressed the hardness of his body against her softness, letting her feel the strength of his desire. He needed this woman to know just how badly he wanted her. How badly he wanted to lay her down in the hay and sate his body with hers. This time his kiss held equal parts desire and pent-up denial. Luke bruised the rosy softness of her lips as he took her with his mouth. Recognizing that he needed to ease his fierce possession her lips, to pull back on his desire before he scared her, he forced himself to retreat, suckling the pretty, pouty flesh of her bruised lips gently with his own. The action drew sounds of pleasure from deep within her throat.

Luke struggled with his conscience as his desire threatened to escalate out of control, almost pushing him past the point of no return. The feel of her small hands on his chest played havoc with his senses. Mary had gotten under his skin and burrowed her way into his heart.

He broke off the bone-melting kiss and buried his head in the soft, smooth skin of her neck, knowing he couldn't continue. Not and keep his sanity.

He cupped her face in the palm of his hands. Her lips were swollen and glistened with moisture. Moisture from his mouth. He silently groaned and almost said to hell with his good intentions. She felt so alive in his arms, so vibrant. And he felt so alive in hers.

Fighting the desire that threatened to overwhelm him, he drew back. He was always in control. Always. He moved away before his animal instincts overcame him.

"You were right. That wasn't such a good idea after all." He grabbed Lucifer's reins and walked into the pouring rain.

CHAPTER FIVE

The next morning Mary rose early, prepared breakfast and hid in her room while Luke and his grandfather ate their meal. She knew she'd taken the coward's way out, but she couldn't face Luke. Not yet. Looking out her bedroom window, she saw him leaning against the dusty pickup that would carry them to town. She watched as he pulled a pack of cigarettes from the pocket of his jacket. He reminded her of the old advertisements on television–a rough and rugged man of the open range. A cowboy through and through. As if sensing her scrutiny, he turned his head and looked into her second story window. Mary quickly moved behind the curtain before he could see her.

God, his kisses yesterday made the memory of every kiss she'd ever had before disappear. And she couldn't believe she'd been so bold! Touching him, tasting him. She'd never felt that kind of desire before.

And he wanted her. She had seen it in his eyes, felt it in his touch. It made her feel as warm and gooey inside as the chocolate chip cookies he loved. And beautiful. It made her feel so beautiful.

Mary knew she couldn't hide in her room forever. She went downstairs, running into Joseph in the hallway.

"Did you sleep well, Mary?" The older man helped her with her coat.

"Fine, Joseph," she lied. She hadn't slept a wink, reliving every moment in the barn over and over again.

"Well, I'm glad someone did," he muttered as he led her out of the house.

"Aren't you sleeping well? Maybe you should talk to Dr. McAllister about that today."

"Not me, darling. That grandson of mine. He was up half the night."

"Did one of the mares go into labor?" On one of their walks Joseph had shared Luke's more recent 'stud' service. Lucifer had covered three of the brood mares in early fall and they were expecting the new arrivals any day.

"No, not yet. I don't know what's wrong with boy. He hasn't slept well for days. He hasn't been this restless since his wife left."

Mary shivered as she imagined Luke spending sleepless nights because of her. She wanted him to need her. To want her to the point of madness. To need her the way he needed his next breath. His passion would be as explosive as–as, well, explosive as the episode in the barn. But hotter.

As they neared the truck, she avoided his gaze. It was bad enough remembering the kisses they had shared, much less the other images her daydreaming mind had created.

"Good morning, Mary." Luke dropped his cigarette and put it out with a sharp movement of his boot.

"Good morning, Luke." She tried to figure out a graceful way to slide into the truck. Granted she was tall, but it took quite a bit of leverage power to hop into the high cab of a ranch truck. As she stepped onto the running board, she felt Luke behind her, his hands helping her ascend. For one exquisite moment, she let herself rely on the strength of his tall body, inhaling the tobacco and leather smells embedded in his jacket, lingering on his skin.

All too soon, she found herself seated between the two men. Mary tried to concentrate on the scenery and not the feel of Luke's hard muscular leg pressing against hers as he drove. She was grateful when Joseph finally spoke.

"When in the blue blazes is someone going to change that confounded sign?" One long finger pecked repeatedly against the window as Joseph pointed to a bright green highway sign that greeted people at the edge of town. Its large white letters proclaimed: Fiddler Creek, Wyoming, population 782. "That census taker was as drunk as the darn fool who founded this town."

Mary laughed at the older man's bluster, grateful for the conversation. The beauty of the country with its far off mountains, plush green grasses and silver blue lakes had enthralled Mary in much the same way it had captured the hearts of the first people to see the valley. And she never tired of hearing about how the town had gotten its name.

Luke gave her an engaging wink that sent tingles down her spine while he encouraged the older man to tell the tale. "Go ahead, Grandpa. I know you're dying to tell Mary your version of the story."

"My version is the true version, young man. And don't you forget it." Joseph glared at this grandson before he continued. "Legend has it that a band of settlers founded the town after they wandered off the wagon trail while heading west."

Mary watched Joseph's face as he told the story. No doubt he visualized the scene in his mind and it startled her to realize that, with his words, she could see it as well.

"With winter already upon them, they looked around and saw the lazy river fed by sweet mountain streams. They saw the wide valley and knew that dark, rich soil lay buried beneath the snow. There was plenty of water and enough room for a man to breathe. Weary and worn, they decided to stay." Joseph encased the whole valley before him with one sweep of his hand.

"To celebrate their new home, the women cooked up the last of their flour and the men went hunting. Every man, woman, and child feasted on biscuits, honey, and wild game. With their bellies full and the fires burning bright and warm, the men tuned up their musical instruments and broke out their stash of corn liquor. One man drank and played his fiddle so long that he passed out dead center of the frozen creek. By the time he woke up the next day, there was no land left for the poor fellow to claim except a small portion next to the creek. And that's how the town got its name." He folded his arms across his chest, a smug smile on his face.

"That's it?" Joseph had told the same tale she'd heard time and time again from all the local residents-the exact same story printed on the brochures that the Chamber of Commerce passed out during the summer months. Luke rewarded her silence with a mouthed thank you, which Mary savored for the remainder of the trip.

Once in town, Luke parked the truck in front of a large brick building that served as the town's city hall. As soon as the truck stopped, Joseph made a beeline across the street to a group of men gathered outside the feed and grain store.

"We're a little early." Luke put out a hand to stop Mary when she started to exit. "Do you need to do anything before Grandpa's appointment?"

She nodded. "I need to get my car from the garage. Jennifer called yesterday and said Eddie had it ready."

"Afraid you're going to be stuck at the ranch without a way to leave? Missing the bright lights already?" His tone was harsh and she saw the glitter of anger in the green depths of his eyes.

"No," she replied stiffly, hurt that he would think something like that after their interlude in the barn.

Was he afraid she didn't like the ranch, didn't like him? Little did he know! "I'm happy at the Circle T, Luke. And your grandfather's been a doll of a patient."

"I'm glad to hear that, Mary. Real glad." He gave her one of his rare smiles and her heart flipped over in her chest. His fingertips trailed along the underside of her jaw and his head bent closer. He was going to kiss her.

A sharp tap on the passenger side window jerked them guiltily apart. "Hey, you two, I'm going over to Smitty's. I'll meet you at Doc Logan's later."

"That's fine, Grandpa. We're headed to Eddie's Garage." He exited the truck then walked around to open Mary's door.

As they walked through town, Luke took her hand and she savored the moment, loving the feel of his fingers entwined with her own. As they walked, he tipped his hat in greeting to people they passed on the street but never let go of her hand.

"You're very popular," she commented, after the mayor had stopped to talk about the weather. The storm of last night had passed–with no snow–but the air was heavy with anticipation. Something was brewing.

"It comes with the territory," Luke said.

"What territory?"

He veered off onto a side street, making his way to Eddie's Garage. "Being rich. Everyone wants to stay on your good side, even if they can't stand the sight of you."

"That's not true," Mary protested.

"Sure it is." Luke's words flowed out of his mouth easily enough, but Mary sensed a hurt behind them.

"Do you really think that's the only reason they speak to you?" she asked.

"I don't think it, honey, I know it is." They had reached the garage. Luke pushed open the battered wooden door and ushered her inside.

"That's not true." Luke was too decent a man for him to think people only wanted to socialize with him simply because of his wealth.

"Isn't that why you came to the Circle T, because you wanted something?"

"Well, yes," she sputtered. "But that's not the same thing.

One black brow arched. "Really?"

"I've talked to you before and never wanted anything."

"When?"

"At the summer camp last year."

"You didn't say a word to me, Mary. You helped with the kids all day if memory serves me right."

"Well, maybe I didn't speak to you." Mary's heart skipped a beat when she realized Luke had noticed her after all. And regretted the fact she hadn't had the courage to talk to him then. "But, did you speak to me?"

"Not that I recall." His frowned deepened.

"See, you're just as bad as you think others are. Wasn't I pretty enough to garner your attention?" She held her breath as she waited for his answer.

Luke stopped and encircled her arm with one large hand, his hold almost bruising in its force. He jerked her toward him. "If I didn't speak to you, it had nothing to do with how you look. You're a very attractive woman."

"Right." Mary didn't believe his words. She knew exactly how she looked beneath her warm winter sweaters. She tried to pull her arm free and walk away. "That's why all those Hollywood directors are knocking down my door with requests for me to star in their next beach movie."

Luke's green eyes narrowed into tiny slits. "Didn't I notice you in the barn yesterday?"

She flushed, heat suffusing her cheeks as she remembered their shared passion. "Well, y-yes," she stammered." But I know it was just the situation. You are a cowboy after all, Mr. Tanner."

"Don't lump me in with a bunch of rough rednecks looking for a good time," he growled. He tugged her flush against his big body. "I'm a man who noticed a very attractive, very desirable woman. Maybe you need a little reminder of that fact." He lowered his head.

Mary waited with baited breath for his mouth to touch hers. Despite her looks and her size, did he find her attractive? She was almost starting to believe it. Almost. Her heart filled with joy at the thought anyway. She stood on her tiptoes, her head lifted and ready to meet his mouth halfway.

"Hi, Ms. Carter."

Mary groaned in regret as Eddie Carson, Jr., son of the owner of Eddie's Garage and its head mechanic, called a greeting from the back of the building, bringing the magic moment to an end. It did her ego worlds of good to hear Luke curse as he dropped his hands and stepped away.

"Your car's ready, ma'am. I'll have one of the boys pull it around front." The mechanic wiped his greasy hands on an even greasier rag. He pulled a clipboard from the wall and totaled her bill. "I don't mean to be bossy, but you really do need a new set of tires. With this cold weather threatening snow again and the spring rains coming soon, you can never be too careful."

She sighed as she read the total bill. There went her plans to use most of the generous salary from the Tanners to play catch up with the outstanding bills and use what remained to make a down payment on a computer system to track the agency's patients and billing, a tedious job she hated doing by hand every month. Then, if Luke did stay true to his word and give her the loan, she would have enough working capital to see her through until next summer. If she were very, very frugal.

She wrote a check to cover the cost of the repairs, kissing the computer goodbye. A car, she desperately needed. A computer, she wanted but could do without for a while longer.

"I know, Eddie. You tell me that every time I bring my car in. You know I do well to keep that old bucket of bolts running, which is due entirely to your expertise." She smiled gratefully at the young mechanic as she handed him the check. Always honest in his dealings with her, both in the repairs and the prices he charged, she knew she would have spent twice as much for half the work in a larger city

"What's wrong with the lady's tires, Carson?"

Mary watched as Luke pulled a pack of cigarettes from his pocket. Before he could flick open his lighter, she pulled it from his hand and tossed it in the garbage, ignoring his muttered curse. She really wished he hadn't asked that question. He wouldn't like the answer.

"Well, sir." Eddie cleared his throat nervously and Mary smiled. Everyone knew Luke Tanner and his legendary temper. But to her amazement, his voice croaked only a little when he spoke. "They're worn out, sir. Balder than a baby's butt."

Luke growled low in his throat at the other man's words and Mary knew what was coming. She shook her finger at him in warning.

"Now don't you look at me like that, mister. You've already scared poor Eddie to death." Even though she started to tremble at the look in his eyes herself, she didn't back down. "I'll get to it when I can."

"Go put some tires on the lady's car, son," He never took his eyes from Mary's face.

Eddie left as fast as he could, giving her no chance to veto Luke's high-handed order.

Mary rounded on the rancher. "And just who do you think is going to pay for those tires?" she demanded as she started after the mechanic. "Santa Claus?"

He grabbed her arm, forcing her to face him. "You need those blasted tires and you're going to have them. Got it?" The expression on his face brooked no argument, but Mary's temper had gone beyond reason.

"I will not," she declared. The man interfered too damned much by putting tires on her car that she couldn't afford.

She wanted to take him to task for his high-handed manner but he was kissing her in the most delightful way.

"There's only one way to deal with a willful woman," he murmured against her mouth as he came up for air. Before she could respond, his mouth once again claimed hers, deepening the kiss.

"Luke," she whispered when he stopped, for once at loss for words. His kiss floored her.

"Say it again," he demanded, touching his forehead to hers.

"Say what again?" she asked, too dazed by his touch to think straight. Boy-oh-boy, could the man kiss.

"My name. Say my name again."

"Luke."

He groaned, a deep aching sound that seemed to come from the very depths of his soul. He kissed her temple. "What am I going to do with you?"

Mary brought her hands to his chest and pushed until he relaxed his hold enough for her to see his face. In his eyes she saw confusion and desire and knew the emotions mirrored the ones simmering deep within her own. It gave her a much-needed shot of courage.

"What would you like to do with me?" she asked. It was almost the same dare she'd voiced the day she'd asked him for a loan.

Mary's knees threatened to buckle at the look of raw hunger that blazed in his eyes and she had to lean back against the wall for support.

"You don't want me to answer that, Mary. Not here. Not now." His voice was low and thick.

"Then where Luke? Where will you tell me?" She licked her lips, savoring the taste of him that still lingered there.

As if her gesture had upset him, he clutched the band of his hat in his hand, ruining the soft gray felt fabric with the strength of his grip. She quivered with excitement.

"At the dance tomorrow," he said. "Come to the dance with me." On a regular basis the little town of Fiddler Creek held dances at the local community center. The populace didn't need a reason to get together and have a good time, just a free Saturday night.

"Okay." Mary barely spoke above a whisper as she answered.

"Fine." He jammed the abused Stetson back on his head. "Tell Eddie to put the tires on my bill. I'll take Grandpa to the doctor. You can go on home once your car is finished."

Luke's gaze swept over her once last, lingering time. "Will you be okay?"

"Yes." Her voice broke. Her heart lurched as he swooped down to claim a hard, forceful kiss before he left.

Mary signed the ticket Eddie handed her once the four new tires were mounted. She vowed to repay Luke just as soon as possible. She knew she should be grateful that he cared enough to worry about her, but her strong streak of independence forced her to make the promise. His concern, however, did give her hope that he wasn't as hardhearted as he appeared. And that he did care about her in some small way. She wasn't fool enough not to realize that the intimacy of living together may be contributing to Luke's sudden show of desire. Not that she was complaining. But she was realistic. Would he look at her in roomful of slender, beautiful women and exhibit the same desire? Probably not.

As she headed out of the garage she had to admit the car drove much better with the new tires. She didn't have to admit that to Luke though. Her grin was happy and excited.

She debated what to do with her unexpected free afternoon. She experienced a twinge of guilt about not being with Joseph for his appointment but knew he wouldn't mind. Dr. McAllister would email her a full report anyway. Besides, she hadn't had any time off since going to work at the Circle T.

Excitement about the upcoming dance skittered along her spine and she thought about visiting Jennifer. But this budding 'something' was too fragile to share even with her best friend. Mary had never felt so alive and so wanted in all her life. She actually had a date with Luke Tanner, the richest man in Fiddler Creek. Not that his status had anything to do with why she had accepted his invitation. No, Mary wanted to go because of the way he made her feel. He could turn her insides to mush with just one look from those emerald green eyes. Luke made her feel beautiful and wanton all at the same time. And she had never felt that way before.

She steered her little compact car onto Main Street and headed to the only ladies apparel store in town. The proprietor carried a wide range of sizes and a variety of styles. Mary decided to buy a new dress for the dance even if she had to eat peanut butter sandwiches with no jelly for the rest of the year to make up the difference in her bank account. She felt like Cinderella getting ready for the ball.

Remembering the dark brooding look in Luke's eyes, she just prayed her carriage wouldn't turn into a pumpkin at midnight.

CHAPTER SIX

*W*oman, thy name is vanity, Mary thought with a wide smile the next evening as she got ready for the big Saturday night dance. She wouldn't be human though, if she didn't admit that at moments like this she longed to look like Cindy Crawford.

Dieting, which always failed, made her miserable. And for years not being that perfect size eight had eaten away at her self-esteem and self-confidence. But thanks to the support and love of friends like Jennifer, she'd realized long ago that beauty was only skin-deep. And tonight she rid herself of even more of those self-defeating thoughts, burying some deep inside and allowing others to flow away, banishing forever their power to hurt her.

With careful hands she removed her new dress from its protective covering. The clothing store had indeed found something special in stock and Mary would be eating peanut butter sandwiches without the jelly *or* the peanut butter for the next year to pay for her purchase, but she didn't care.

Almost reverently she slipped the midnight blue velvet dress over her head. It had a low neckline and fit like a second skin from the top of her well-rounded breasts to the slight indentation of her waist. From there its full skirt billowed out, hiding a multitude of sins for which Mary gave her eternal thanks. The dress had been designed to make a woman feel wild and reckless. And that's just how she'd been feeling lately.

Ever since Luke Tanner had kissed her senseless in the barn.

She reached for the zipper that ran up her back, her arms stretched as far as they could as she tried to close the zipper. It didn't work. Knowing she would have to have help, she walked down the hall and knocked on Joseph's door.

"Will you come help me for a minute, Joseph?" she called through the door. When she heard a grunt she walked away, slipping back into her room.

As she waited for Joseph, she checked her appearance in the mirror one last time pleased at the result. She had applied her makeup with a bit more daring than usual, using eyeliner, blush and silky blue eye shadow a shade darker than her dress. She'd left her hair loose, remembering the compliments Luke had paid her. It brushed the tops of her bare shoulders. Normally she would try to hide her arms, but for once she didn't care about the expanse of skin showing. She wanted the whole world to see Mary Carter, big and beautiful. If someone saw something they didn't like, they could look the other way.

"What are you doing here?" Mary gasped as Luke's reflection joined hers in the silver-backed mirror.

He stood behind her – tall, dark and silent, a cigarette dangling between two lean fingers. He took several draws before he crossed the room to stab it out in the crystal trinket dish on her dresser. Mary couldn't suppress her shudder when his shoulder brushed hers.

"Joseph said you needed some help," he said in a low lazy drawl. His gaze raked across the tops of her exposed breasts. "Let me get you free."

Without waiting for permission, he proceeded to zip up her dress. Mary shivered again when his neatly trimmed fingernails scraped the creamy skin of her spine as he worked the tangled fabric free. Moments later she felt the reassuring pressure as he fastened her dress.

"Thank you." She turned to face him. "I can manage from here."

"You are so beautiful." His eyes darkened as he spoke.

She shook her head denying his words.

"You are beautiful," he insisted. "Firm and soft and silky to the touch."

"Please," she whispered, whether to beg for the kiss shining in his eyes or to ask him to leave she did not know.

Luke laughed, his face taunt. "Please what, Mary? Please stop wanting you? Please stop aching for you? I wish to God I could." Turning on his heel, he strode from the room, slamming the door as he left.

Mary bowed her head and took several gulps of air, resting her shaking hands on the edge of the ornate dresser. She could no longer deny her feelings for the hard-nosed rancher. The first time she'd seen Luke, even from a distance, she'd felt a deep, sensual pull as old as time itself. And the past month and a half had only brought home to her just how much she cared for the silent man who would never be more than just her boss.

Innocent and inexperienced though she was, she knew Luke desired her and would probably enter into an affair if she gave him the slightest encouragement. But Mary wanted more. She wanted someone to love her always, someone to spend her life with. And that someone would not be Luke Tanner. He was too bitter, to heart sore to see the life they could have together.

She sighed with regret for things that would never be and gathered her purse. She was determined to enjoy this night no matter what.

Cars crowded the parking lot at the community center. Music floated through the air and the sound of people having a wonderful time could be heard for miles around.

The only blemish on the night was the slight rain that continued to fall. But even that could not put a damper on the festivities. The local high school Beta Club members, armed with oversized umbrellas, had volunteered to escort the partygoers from their cars to the doorway and everyone arrived happy and dry.

The citizens of Fiddler Creek and the surrounding county enjoyed these community get-togethers. Some waited anxiously until their sweethearts asked them to the dance, while others looked forward to perhaps starting something new and exciting.

Men dressed in tuxedos escorted women draped in faux diamonds and pearls. Much to Mary's surprise just as many were dressed in denim and polyester. She could have worn her jeans and sweater and no one would have paid the least bit of attention. The soft swirl of satin-lined velvet against her legs made her glad she had dressed up. After all, Cinderella only went to the ball once.

"There's a buffet line over there." Luke pointed to three large tables laden with desserts and finger foods that surrounded the dance floor. The array would see the partygoers through the long evening hours and even until early morning. She'd given the Circle T's contribution to the dance committee yesterday. "You might want to get something to eat. You barely touched your dinner."

Mary's heart raced at his observation, taking it as another small sign of concern for her welfare. "I was too nervous. I've never been comfortable in large crowds. I guess that's why I've never attended one of these dances before."

Luke frowned. "If you'd rather leave, I'll take you home and then come back for grandfather later." Even though they had all driven to the dance together, Joseph had excused himself the moment they'd arrived.

Mary's spine stiffened with hurt pride. It seemed Luke had changed his mind and didn't want to be there–at least not with her. She might have known her fairy tale night would turn into a tale from the Brothers Grimm.

"If you want to leave, go ahead. I'll be fine." She held her head high and her shoulders straight. She'd been rejected before. It would only hurt for a little while. At least that's what she told herself.

Luke cursed and pulled her to the back of the room. "Look, Mary," he said, his mouth a thin line of anger. "I don't want you to leave and I don't want to leave. You've got me so tied up in knots I don't know if I'm coming or going. You're nothing like the other women I've dated."

"Oh." Mary felt crushed at his words and her world came crashing down around her ears all over again. But she didn't let him see the pain. "You don't think I'm pretty enough or slim enough to be seen with you, right?"

"Damn it, Mary," Luke growled. "That's not what I meant. Someone did a number on you didn't they?"

She shrugged. "Maybe."

Luke moved closer. "Who was it?"

She laughed, the sound just short of being hysterical. "It would be easier to list who it wasn't."

"You have no confidence in your ability to please a man, do you? You have no idea just how beautiful you are."

"I'm not beautiful, Luke. I wish you would stop saying that."

"Maybe if I say it enough, you'll start to believe me. Maybe if I show you how much you make me want you, you'll do something about it. What do you say, Mary? Care to prove you're *not* a desirable woman?" His tone was challenging at best, belligerent at most.

But for once Mary refused to rise to the bait.

"Please, Mary. I want to dance with you tonight. I want to feel my arms around you even if it is in the middle of a damn crowd."

Mary wanted to stay more than anything. To stay in his arms forever. To receive the promises she saw glittering in his green eyes. She knew her time with him was limited and knew when she did walk away, her heart would stay behind.

"So, you're asking me out?" she teased, making up her mind to seize the moment.

Luke grinned and nodded his head.

"Then as your date," she emphasized the last word with a small, shy smile. "I think it's only fair to warn you, I'm starving. Let's eat." She took his hand and marched him to the buffet line. The appetite which had deserted her earlier at the ranch returned in full. After they filled their plates, Luke led her to a quiet corner.

"Shouldn't we join Joseph?" She took her seat, secretly delighted that he had chosen a table away from the crowd.

"Afraid to be alone with me?" A mischievous spark danced in his hooded eyes.

"I don't know. Are you going to turn into a big, bad wolf?"

"The way you look tonight, you never know, darlin'." His eyes lingered on the swells of her breasts. "You never know."

Mary's heart sang. "I just thought it would be rude of us not to join him."

"Don't worry about Granddad, he's okay. He's with Sara." He pointed to the far corner where his grandfather sat with a dark haired woman a few years his junior. Luke went on to explain that the two had been dating on and off for over a year.

"Are you sure that's all you want?" He nodded at her plate.

Mary had filled her plate with chocolate covered strawberries and nothing else. "I guess I kind of went overboard, didn't I? But it's Jennifer's fault. These are her specialty and they're delicious. Have you ever had one?"

Luke shook his head. "But don't let me stop you. Go ahead and eat." He took one from her plate and held it to her mouth.

Mesmerized, she sank her teeth into the red, ripe flesh. The rich creamy chocolate blended perfectly with the berry's sweetness. As she finished the luscious treat, she licked the excess juice from her lips.

"You taste one." She held out large berry.

Almost savagely, he bit the fruit in half. The juice ran down her hand. Before she could grab a napkin, Luke brought her hand to her mouth and licked her fingers–one at a time. A heaviness settled low in her stomach and a delicious warmth flooded her insides.

A blare of music signaled the start of the dance and the floor filled up quickly. Mary pushed the last of her food away, her heart pounding too fast to finish. Unconsciously, her toe started tapping to the beat of the music.

Luke stared at her. The look in his eyes made her nervous. When would he ask her to dance? Would it be a fast dance or a slow dance? It would feel like heaven to be in his arms.

"Let's go." He pushed his chair back. The metal legs scraped against the concrete floor.

Just as they reached the dance floor, the band switched to a soft melody, perfect for a slow dance. Luke guided them around the floor with surprising grace for such a big man. Mary sighed happily as she clung to his hand and savored the feel of his body pressed against hers.

"Did I tell you how beautiful you looked tonight?" he whispered in her ear.

"Luke," she protested. "I thought we'd settled that."

"I thought we had, too." He moved until he could see her eyes. "I thought you were going to listen when I spoke."

Mary had the grace to blush. "Alright, lay it on, mister. Tell me what a raving beauty I am and how much you want me."

Luke smiled, a predatory smile if ever Mary saw one, and she knew she had gone too far. He pulled her close, letting her feel exactly what she did to him. "Do you feel me, Mary? Do you feel how much I want you?" He ground his hips against her soft belly. As the next song started, he swung them off the dance floor and into a small alcove off to the side.

"Mary." Her name was a mere whisper of breath as he brushed her mouth with his. His fingers stroked the nape of her neck under the weight of her hair.

"Open your mouth for me, baby. Just like that day in the barn." He bit into the soft tender flesh of her bottom lip, and she cried out in pleasure. Heat engulfed her and she pressed herself against his hard form, breathing in his warm, male scent.

He muttered something low and rough, breaking off the kiss. His hands roamed over the flesh of her arms, the sides of her waist and explored the soft outer curves of her breasts. She trembled, but didn't pull away or protest. Her blood heated with delicious anticipation. Holding her stare, he brushed his thumbs across the puckered centers. For long, endless moments he caressed her, his eyes darkening with an indefinable emotion before a shuttered expression settled over his rough features.

He placed her hand on the bugle in front of his charcoal gray pants and urged her to cup him with her palm. Mary's moan mingled with his as she closed her fingers around him, squeezing ever so slightly. "I want to make you wet with wanting, Mary. So wet that you can take me with a single stroke."

He raised her hand to her mouth, kissing her trembling fingers "Don't ever think I don't want you, baby. Don't ever think you're not beautiful."

"I won't," Mary whispered, a part of her finally beginning to believe his words.

"I know all this is new for you, Mary." He toyed with a strand of her hair. The pale silver color seemed to fascinate him.

Hectic color flooded Mary's face. "Yes."

"It's relatively new to me, too," Luke admitted. "But I don't expect you to believe that."

"I know you were married." She was reluctant to bring up any subject that might shatter this fragile moment.

Luke gave a short bark of laughter. "Yeah, for all of two minutes." For a brief instant, Mary sensed his need to talk, to share his feelings. She held her breath and waited. The moment passed and he patted the pockets of his suit until he found his pack of cigarettes. She took them from him and tossed them on a table.

"Smartass." He groused but grinned at her. "Go inside and find grandfather. I need a few moments alone."

"Will you kiss me again, Luke?"

"Hell, Mary, what do you think I'm made of, steel?"

"Apparently so." Her eyes went to the front of his pants that hadn't lost any of their fullness. He scrubbed his hand along his jaw.

His touch held a measure of male possession and an unspoken warning when he lifted her against him to kiss her so thoroughly and hungrily that she gasped when he let her go.

Without another word, he gave her a not-so-gentle pat on her swaying backside and sent her on her way. Mary stopped at the edge of the dance floor, turning back to watch as he stepped into the rain swept night. She knew she might be reading more than he intended into what they had shared, but she wanted to go after him, to stay with him until the world faded away. But she knew she couldn't.

A sudden silence fell over the group as she joined Joseph and his date. Joseph's knowing look made her blush. "He had to go outside for a few minutes."

"He's smoking those damned cigarettes again," Joseph huffed.

"No, he's not. I took them away from him." Mary took a seat beside her patient.

"Good for you, Mary. I want you to meet my Sara." He introduced the woman by his side and Mary could see something special existed between the two older people.

"I've heard so much about you," the other woman said. Her warm and infectious smile had Mary responding instantly. The two exchanged pleasantries and Mary soon discovered Sara had retired from nursing only the year before. As they continued to talk, Mark and Jennifer walked up with a fretful baby Jessica in tow.

"Let me take her, honey." Mark shifted the fussy child into his arms.

Jennifer sighed as the baby continued to cry despite her husband's ministrations. "I guess she needs to be changed. And fed. Will you come with me, Mary? I hate to walk to the restrooms by myself. I don't know why they put them so far away from the main hall."

"Of course," Mary agreed. She tried not to look for Luke.

Joseph squeezed her arm as she passed. "When he comes back, I'll tell him where you went."

"Thanks." Mary smiled. No point in trying to hide it now. Anyone who had seen them at the table sharing the chocolate treat or making their way to the dark corner of the hall would have guessed her true feelings for Luke Tanner.

Once inside the ladies room, Jennifer changed the baby's soiled diaper and took a seat in one of the leather chairs in the alcove. "There, that's all that was wrong with my little girl." She lowered the front of her dress and settled the infant in her arms to nurse.

"How are you enjoying the dance? Did Luke like my strawberries?"

Mary fussed with her hair as she stared at her reflection in the mirror. Sometimes having a best friend who knew you so well could be very annoying.

"Don't clam up on me now," Jennifer begged. "I want details."

"You're a married woman. What kind of details can I possibly give you?"

"I'm married, not dead, for heaven's sake. Come on, give," she growled.

Mary shook her head. "There's nothing to tell. We ate a little and danced a little."

The other woman became serious. "Did you talk any?"

"Some, but Luke isn't much of a talker."

It was Jennifer's turn to shake her head. "Darling, I know you don't want to hear this, but…"

"You're right. I don't want to hear it. You got lucky, Jennifer. Mark is a wonderful man who loves you to distraction."

"I didn't mean to upset you. I just don't want you rushing into anything, doing something you'll regret later." Her eyes filled with sympathy and Mary knew her friend had guessed her feelings for Luke without being told. And her intentions should the opportunity ever arise. Remembering the feel of him beneath her hand had her insides clenching.

"I'm never going to have what you have. I've accepted that about myself and my life. But if I can have a night with this man holding me close, I'll take it. Happily-ever-after never happens for women like me." She sighed in regret. "I'm staying until Joseph's cast comes off and then I'll have my loan and forget all about Luke Tanner."

They shared a sad smile and left the restroom, returning to the dance.

When Mary and Jennifer returned to the party, they discovered Luke had received a urgent call from the ranch informing him that one of his pregnant mares might be in trouble. He'd hitched a ride and left the truck for Joseph and Mary. They stayed until the early hours of the morning but for Mary, the night had lost its fairy tale feeling.

Suddenly she felt just like Cinderella had after the ball–pumpkin coach, rats and all.

CHAPTER SEVEN

A few days later, Luke shifted restlessly in his saddle and tried to find a comfortable position on the cold wet leather. He'd given up any hope of staying dry in the deluge now falling. He cursed each cold drop of rain that found its way beneath his weatherproof poncho. For hours he had ridden through the unrelenting downfall and there seemed to be no relief in sight.

Another cow escaped from the herd and he wheeled Lucifer around to catch the errant animal. Tired and damp, he just wanted to go the hell home. He and his men had been up since before dawn moving cattle across the waterlogged plains.

The cattle had to be rounded up and moved to the mountain pastures pronto. He didn't care what the weatherman said, the town of Fiddler Creek, as well as his ranch, was in for a good old-fashioned flooding.

He urged his stallion forward and headed for the mountains. More than one cow had already strayed through the boundary fence he had repaired earlier that week. Or thought he had repaired. He winced. His mind had been more on Mary than the job at hand. She had him so confused, he was behaving like some greenhorn kid.

Luke cursed roundly as the clouds above him broke open again drenching him all the way through in spite of his waterproof poncho. It was nothing more than he deserved he thought as he tugged the collar of his slicker up around his neck. Why shouldn't the fates decree their displeasure with him?

The past few weeks had been both heaven and hell. Every time he looked at Mary his heart thudded and a little more of his soul thawed. He wanted this woman with a blinding need that increased with each passing day. The torture of wanting her and not being able to have all of her sweetness drove him mad.

But something, some deep buried sense of honor kept him from taking her. He knew that more than one woman had been swept away by passion, only to regret the hot savage flames once they cooled. The essence of goodness, she represented everything his life lacked. More, she looked at him as though she would stay with him forever if he asked.

And during these last few weeks, Luke realized he no longer wanted a flash in the pan romance. He wanted a deep, lasting relationship like the one his great-grandparents had shared and what he had seen between Joseph and Emma.

At the dance he'd almost went down on one knee and asked Mary to run off to Vegas and marry him that very night. But then he'd overheard her conversation with Jennifer. She was leaving as soon as she got the loan.

Just like his ex-wife, she'd be gone as soon as the ink dried on the check. He guessed he should be grateful that she had spared him the bedroom scene, even though heaven knew he'd have no problem consummating his relationship with Mary. Damn it to hell, he wanted the woman badly. His hands tightened into fists, jerking the reins. The horse danced sideways.

"Sorry boy." He patted Lucifer's neck in apology. He raised his face to the sky and allowed the rain to pour over his face as he breathed in the clean, rain-soaked air. Maybe he could somehow purge his soul and ease the constant ache in his heart.

He hunched his shoulders. He was cold, wet and very, very angry. None of which would get the job done. He urged his mount forward and forced thoughts of Mary from his mind. "Come on, Lucifer, we've got a lot more to do today."

Mary removed the last towel from the dryer and added it to the stack on top of the machine. She gathered them in her arms and walked into the adjoining kitchen. A jagged streak of lightening lit the darkened sky and she nearly jumped out of her skin when someone pounded on the back door at the same time. She turned, the warm towels held to her chest like a shield.

"Hawk." She sagged with relief and opened the screen to let the foreman inside. "You scared me half to death. And this storm is horrible."

The tall man remained standing just inside the door. He didn't even help himself to one of the fresh-from-the-oven cookies sitting on the counter. Almost from the very first day of her arrival, Mary had taken to supplementing Rooster's less than imaginative fare with cakes, pies and cookies. She had earned the friendship and admiration of every cowboy on the ranch. Especially Hawk.

But today the man stood silently, dripping a puddle of water on the shiny tile floor and twisting the brim of his hat with nervous fingers.

"What's wrong?" She tightened her hold on the towels. "Oh, my God, it's Joseph. Something's happened to Joseph." She hadn't seen the older man since early in the morning when he'd gone to help the boys in the barn. Mary would never forgive herself if something had happened to the older gentlemen. Not only had Luke trusted her to look after him, but Joseph himself had managed to earn an important place in her heart.

"No, ma'am," Hawk reassured her. "Joseph is fine. He's in the barn with Naomi, the soon-to-be mama." Another of Circle T's prize mares was about to give birth to Lucifer's offspring. Luke had shared with her his hope that the mare's gentle breeding would be a calming factor in stallion's otherwise fiery prodigy.

"Then what?" She fought the strong sense of anxiety that overtook her and put the towels aside.

"It's Luke, Mary. Lucifer just rode in without him."

She clutched the back of the kitchen chair, her knuckles whitened with the strength of her grip. "What do you think happened?" She forced the words past a suddenly tight throat.

"Well, ma'am." Hawk hesitated and she wanted to grab him by the shirt and yank the words from his mouth. Instead she willed herself to wait.

"I don't think he'll be hurt bad, nothing 'cept maybe his pride. Lucifer probably just got spooked by this lightening and threw him. He has a tendency to do that during a storm. He's a dang ornery critter."

Mary wanted to scream at him to stop giving her a rundown on the horse's attitude. Luke could be out there somewhere badly injured, despite what Hawk said. "Shouldn't someone be out looking for him?"

"That's why I came up to the house." The battered hat began another round through nervous fingers.

"Yes?" She lost what little patience she'd managed to maintain.

"Well, you see, Luke ordered all of the men to roundup strays up around Fiddler Range. It'd take a good hour to get a message to 'em. There's no phone reception out there. And, well, I can't leave Naomi while she's so close to delivering, it being a breech. Joseph can't do it alone, on account of his arm and all. Luke would skin me alive if I let something happen to that foal."

Mary caught his drift and so did not like where this was headed." You want me to go look for Luke? I can't ride in this storm, Hawk. I barely know how."

"Now, Mary." He spoke with the gentle patience he'd use to speak to a frightened horse. "You've been practicing nearly every day this month." After that very first lesson, Luke had ordered Hawk to be her instructor. "And you've got a fine seat. If I didn't think you'd do just fine, I'd never ask you to go. Luke would grind me into a bloody pulp if I let anything happen to you."

As he spoke, lightening crackled again. The sky opened up and torrents of rain spilled to the ground. The already saturated soil became a river of mud. Seconds later thunder boomed. The sound vibrated throughout the house and rattled the windows. Mary hated storms. As a child she'd hidden in her room, blinds drawn, until they passed.

But what if Luke was injured? What if he was hurt, somewhere out in the open, unprotected against the storm's fury? She stopped. She mustn't allow herself to think such thoughts. She had to keep a clear, calm head and think rationally. "You're right, Hawk. I need to go. Saddle Lady Jane for me. I'll change and get the first aid kit and then be right out."

Hawk strode out of the door before she'd even finished speaking.

In her room, Mary quickly donned thick socks, jeans and a long sleeved shirt. Pulling her hair atop her head, she secured the thick mass into a ponytail and slipped on her boots. Her movements quick and efficient, she gathered the first aid kit from Luke's bathroom. She tore out of the house like the hounds of hell nipped at her heels.

The entire process, clothes changed and supplies gathered, took less than five minutes, but she still felt as though she moved in slow motion. In the barn, she hugged Joseph goodbye.

He held the reins for several seconds, his wrinkled brow puckered in concentration. "Are you sure you want to go, Mary? That grandson of mine can take care of himself."

She was touched by the older man's show of concern. "I'll be fine, Joseph. And I'll find Luke."

"I know you will, Mary. And don't try to make it back until this storm passes. Go to the old line shack and hole up. There's a radio there and Luke can call the barn so we'll know you're alright."

"Will do." She guided the horse from the barn and into the slashing rain. Digging in her heels, she spurred the sturdy animal into a bone-rattling run.

Mary rode away from the storm and by the time she reached her destination the rain had settled into a light drizzle. Hawk had given her clear directions to where Luke was supposed to be working. From the top of a small knoll, she spotted him. The flood-tide of relief she felt left her weak. For several seconds, she could only stare. He moved with his usual loose limbed gait over the rough terrain. He reminded her of Lucifer, big and muscled, arrogant and dangerous. Oh, so dangerous to the inexperienced rider. Or the inexperienced woman.

Mary urged the red sorrel forward. She knew Luke would not be in a good mood.

And she was right.

"What in the hell are you doing out here?"

Tiny drops of water dripped from the ends of his hair jutting from beneath his Stetson. He'd removed his shirt, which revealed a thickly grown layer of hair over a smooth layer of silk. The muscles of his upper body were stunningly defined, his shoulders broad and strong, made to lean upon. His stomach didn't have the washboard smoothness of a male model. His muscles came from the hard physical work of running a ranch, not the results of hours spent in the gym. A hard working man who needed good, solid food to see him through the day. His healthy lifestyle showed on his fame.

As she stared, a rivulet of water followed the natural contours of his body until it disappeared into the waistband of his jeans, drawing Mary's eyes with it. His sodden jeans clung to his male curves. Breathless, she dragged her eyes back to his face, which matched the thunderclouds overhead.

"I came to rescue you." She tried her best to keep her voice even, though laughter swelled in her chest. She could understand how he might feel a little out of sorts.

"Your horse came back without you. We thought you might be hurt," she went on to explain when he just stood there, not saying a word.

Luke snorted, his hands on his hips in an aggressive stance. "Lady, nobody should have come out in a storm like this. And especially not a greenhorn like you. There's liable to be flash floods. If you were one of my hands, I'd fire your ass for pulling a stunt like this." He glared at her, his brows drawn together in a fierce scowl.

She looked down at him from her perch high atop her horse. "Well, I'm not one of your hands and you can't fire me. We have deal, remember? But if you stand there much longer, I might just leave your ass out here in the rain, since you seem to like it so much."

Her words seemed to deflate his anger a little. He removed his hat and raked his fingers through his sodden hair. "Damn it, Mary, you shouldn't have come."

He swung himself into the saddle behind her and the laughter died in the back of her throat at the feel of his heavily muscled chest at her back. Suddenly Mary felt as out of sorts as Luke looked.

"Somebody had to," she pointed out, more than a little breathless from his close proximity. Mary knew having to accept her help irritated the hell out of him.

"This is no job for a woman. I hired you to look after Joseph, not play cowhand. Why didn't Hawk come if all of you were so all fired worried?"

"Naomi's in labor. He thought there'd be hell to pay if he left." Mary struggled to suppress her gasp of pleasure as his arms closed around her. Despite his soaking, he was warm and rock solid. So wonderfully alive.

"He was right," Luke said, and she could see he admitted it grudgingly. "That animal is going to be Lucifer's finest offspring yet. A real champion."

"What happened to your rain gear?" She tried to turn in the saddle but the tightening of his arms stopped her. He buried his cold face against the side of her neck. A moment passed before he whispered.

"I lost it."

"How did you lose a slicker–and a shirt?"

"Believe me, honey, it wasn't easy." He took the reins of the red sorrel and clicked his tongue. The horse surged forward. In minutes, they reached the top of another knoll and Mary had her answer.

"He stole them." Luke pointed to a small white and red calf chewing on a yellow raincoat that matched the one she wore.

Mary laughed.

"You find that funny?" Luke bit out sarcastically.

"Yes, yes, I do," Mary didn't want to reveal the true source of her happiness. "But I still don't understand how he got them."

"In case you missed it, there's a mud hole the size of the Grand Canyon down there. I wasn't about to spend the whole day wet and muddy after I rescued the ungrateful thing, so I took them off."

"And he stole them?"

"Yeah, he stole them." Luke's dark gaze dared her to say more.

"I hate to be the one to tell you this, Luke, but I don't see your shirt anywhere." This time Mary had the good sense to smother her laughter.

"What? That's my lucky poker shirt!"

"Maybe you can get it later," she suggested.

"We'll find it now." Luke urged the horse down the steep incline.

"Wait," she protested. "We need to get you someplace warm and dry, not worry about a shirt. A shirt can be replaced, but you can't."

"Hell," he muttered." You're half frozen."

Mary didn't have the heart to tell him she felt as snug as a bug in a rug because his big body provided more warmth than any heating stove ever had. The shiver stemmed from something much more fundamental than rain and wind.

"Did you tell Joseph we'd come straight back?" Luke shifted in the saddle.

"He told me to head to the line shack if the storm got too bad. He said it had a shortwave." Mary grasped the saddle horn, desperate to keep herself away from the press of his hard body. Away from temptation.

"That's a smart man, my grandfather," Luke murmured, his breath a warm breeze across her ear.

A lump of anticipation settled in the pit of Mary's stomach as he headed north. Away from civilization. Away from everything and everyone. She shivered again and savored the warmth of his breath on her neck. It wouldn't hurt to enjoy him for just a moment, would it? No one said anything had to happen. They'd go to the line shack, spend an hour or so waiting out the storm and be back to the ranch before sundown. She leaned into his embrace and his arms pressed her, if possible, even closer.

Both were instantly, sizzlingly aware that only a few thin layers of wet cloth stood between them. Between them and heaven.

He shifted the reins into one hand while the other tilted her face up to his. "You are so damn beautiful."

Luke slipped his hand inside her yellow slicker and Mary shuddered as he found her swollen nipple. He plucked the large, swollen nub with his calloused fingers, playing it like a fine musical instrument.

"I want you Mary. God how I want you." He moved his hand, splaying his fingers against the curve of her generous hips. Slowly, torturously, he lowered his hand, skimming past the snap of her jeans to briefly touch the part of her that wanted him most.

He shifted their weight and pressed her backside against his aching need. His mouth closed over hers and his tongue nudged her lips apart. Mary was lost. She didn't stop him as he kissed her with savage need. She couldn't. She wanted Luke Tanner more than she wanted to draw her next breath. She opened her mouth, accepting without question his complete and total control. She matched him stroke for stroke, their mating tongues a sweet prelude to what they both knew was to come.

CHAPTER EIGHT

Nothing more than a tumbled down one-room shed, the line shack sat at an odd angle, the whitewashed planks leaning in the direction of the blowing wind. Practically built into the side of the mountain, it had withstood years of abusive weather.

Luke dismounted first. He helped her from the saddle and held her upright until she found her balance. "Go on in. I'll take care of Lady Jane."

Mary nodded, reluctantly tearing her eyes from his perfect physique. He epitomized everything she had ever wanted in a man. And so much more. Shaky legs carried her inside the tiny dwelling that proved to be much roomier than she would have believed.

A blackened, pot-bellied stove sat in the center and served as both a source of heat and the means by which a meal could be prepared. A rickety wooden table with two chairs and an old fashioned tin cabinet, more rust than white, completed the so-called kitchen. The room housed only one other item of furniture, the biggest bed she'd ever seen. Determinedly she turned her back on the inviting softness.

Now shivering in earnest, she removed her wet slicker and equally sodden shoes. A box of matches lay on the shelf above the stove and a stack of kindling rested on the floor. She soon coaxed a small flicker into a roaring fire and the pleasant warmth quickly scattered the chill in the air.

She held her hands to the greedy flames and closed her eyes. Immediately an image of Luke imposed itself on the backs of her closed lids. The kiss they'd shared on the back of the horse had left little doubt that he wanted her. She'd felt the fine tremor in his hands as he'd held her and heard the raggedness of his breathing as they rode.

But Lord help her, she didn't know what to do. If he offered, should she take the passion in the dark of the night, or hold out for her heart's desire and find herself still alone and lonely come the morning light?

One thing was perfectly clear, she loved Luke Tanner.

But she wanted the whole enchilada–home, hearth, family, and yes, the passion filled nights. She wanted the world.

"Oh, Lord, which way is right?" she muttered out loud, more confused than she'd ever been in her entire life.

"What did you say?" Luke closed the door, shutting out the now driving rain.

The sight of him, all muscled, shiny wet, and provocatively male, sent more shivers shooting through her. She licked dry lips. "Um, I said we need some light."

Luke hung his hat by the door and joined her at the stove. "I'm sure there are candles or lanterns around here somewhere. I'm going to radio the ranch and tell them we're safe."

Grateful for any activity that would take her mind off the conflicting feelings he could so easily arouse, she made a quick survey of the cabinet's contents. She found candle stubs, a tin of saltine crackers and several packages of dehydrated vegetable soup.

"Well, at least we won't starve," she said as he finished his conversation with his grandfather. The mare was still in labor but Joseph thought everything would be alright. He told them not to chance coming home until morning.

"Don't go looking like that," Luke laughed as she opened the tin and took a cautious bite, grimacing at the stale taste.

"Like what?"

"As if you'd like to take a bite out of something else."

Mary quirked an eyebrow. "Hmm, not a bad idea. I'd give anything for a big piece of steak right now. Even raw."

He smiled at her savage expression. "If worse comes to worse, I'll go get our well-fed friend and we'll have a barbecue."

"Luke Tanner," she gasped." You wouldn't dare!"

"No," his eyes twinkled. "I wouldn't, but at least I made you smile."

"Why shouldn't I smile?"

"Exactly my point. You're alone in a cabin, miles from anywhere, with the richest man in the county. Most women would give their eyeteeth to be in your position. What more could you want?" He wiggled his eyebrows suggestively.

What more indeed? Mary thought as he searched the upper cabinets she hadn't been able to reach. Maybe a wedding ring and a dark haired baby boy.

"A working commode would be nice." She was amazed at how normal her voice sounded.

"Well, you can't have everything in life."

"Don't I know it," she mumbled. Luke Tanner could have any woman he wanted. Why should he want plain, overweight Mary Carter?

A moment late he held up a battered tin coffee can. "We're in business, darling. I'll get us some water before I change. No sense getting wet again."

Full darkness had fallen by the time he returned. "I'm glad we decided to head here instead of going home. That rain's freezing. While this water boils, I suggest we get out of these wet clothes."

At her startled gasp, she saw his lips twitch in sardonic amusement. "Unless you prefer to catch pneumonia, sweetheart."

Mary clutched the neck of her wet shirt. She had never let a man see her completely naked before, not even her doctor. While comfortable with her size and shape in general, she was not prepared to bare herself to Luke's eyes and show him each and every imperfection of her flesh. Not yet anyway, she told herself honestly. And she knew when–or if–she did, it would be an act of commitment on her part.

Trying to cover her nervousness, she blurted out the first thing that came to mind, moaning as soon as the words left her mouth. "You don't seem in any hurry to take off your pants."

He stilled, the candlelight cast a devilish gleam in his dark green eyes as he reached for the snap of his jeans. "Anytime you're ready, lady. Anytime."

She cleared her clogged throat and glanced around wildly. "Is there someplace I can change?"

After several heat filled seconds, he flicked his hand, indicating a room to the side. "The necessity's over there. I'll see if I can find something for us to wear while you dry off."

Mary hurried inside the small room and stood with her back pressed against the rough plank door. To her, sex was more than a joining of two bodies. It required the blending of souls. Was Luke ready for that kind of commitment?

Just a few shards of light appeared around the edges of the door. She hadn't thought to bring a candle with her. She'd been in too much of a hurry to escape the temptation presented by Luke Tanner. But she had no place to flee. Now she shivered in the darkness, stark naked, with a half-dressed man on the other side of a flimsy wooden door. Some improvement.

"Mary?"

She jumped at the knock on the door.

"I found us something to wear." The door opened and his long, tanned arm appeared inside, a flannel shirt dangled from his fingers.

"Thanks." She grabbed the garment and slammed the door shut, barely missing his knuckles as he moved his hand out of the way. His soft chuckle mocked her haste and the reason for it.

She clenched the plaid material to her breast and willed the tremors in her body to go away.

"Uh, Mary?"

"What?"

"Would you like a candle?"

She opened the door just a crack and a candle and the box of matches came through. "Thanks."

"Anytime, sweetheart. Any time."

She lit the candle and took stock of her surroundings. A chipped enamel sink stood against the outside corner of the room with a battered chamber pot wedged beneath it. A stack of rough looking towels lay folded on a lone pine shelf. She used one to give herself a rub down before donning the borrowed clothes. She thrust her arms into the sleeves of the shirt he had given her. The cuffs completely engulfed her hands. The garment must have been left behind by a big man, because it covered her from neck to mid-thigh. Thank God.

Her legs did not make the most attractive picture in the world or so Mary thought. She had learned long ago that the right clothing could hide a multitude of sins–especially her over abundant thighs. Oh, well, not even her fairy godmother could change her now.

She picked up the candle and left the bathroom. Luke warmed himself by the stove.

"It feels good to be dry, doesn't it?" He'd changed into a pair of dry jeans too. He took her wet clothes and hung them on a nail by the stove next to his.

"Yes, it does." Mary tugged again at the bottom of the shirt as he turned around. Awareness flared between them and the air sizzled with a degree of desire previously unknown to Mary.

Unable to hold his heated gaze she turned away. He had accomplished a lot while she'd hidden in the bathroom. Two bowls and spoons sat on the surface of the well-worn table.

"I guess the next thing we need to do is eat." He turned to the stove where the tin of water boiled.

She watched as he added the soup packets to the water and carried the fare to the table. Unnerved by his blatant maleness, she sat down and focused her attention on the soup in front of her. Not her brightest of moves. Now his broad chest filled her vision.

"Eat up, honey. It won't bite you."

"Would you stop doing that?" Mary snapped. She was overwhelmed by the feelings that flooded her mind and body.

"Doing what?" Luke looked perplexed, his spoon poised half way to his mouth.

"You know what." She slapped her spoon against the table with a loud clank. "Don't you know how demeaning that is?"

Luke lowered his own spoon and placed it beside his bowl.

The action only served to inflame Mary's already volatile temper. A temper caused by hormones raging out of control every time she looked at him. She leaned toward him, unmindful of the way the simple action caused her shirt to gape open, giving him an unrestricted view of her ample charms.

"Um, sweetheart, I don't think, you should…"

"That's the problem with your whole gender, Luke Tanner. You never think. At least not with your brain."

"And just what in your estimable opinion, do we men use to do our thinking?"

Mary glared at him, hating herself for wanting to give into the humor twinkling in his eyes. She didn't know why she had gotten so angry. Oh yeah, the little inner voice reminded her. You're alone with the man you love and you're very, very afraid.

"You know," she sputtered, determined to hang on to the last shred of her ire. She hoped it would save her from an embarrassing situation.

Luke leaned back in his chair.

Mary's eyes followed his movements, lingering with mouth-watering approval on each bulging bicep.

"You think it's demeaning for a man to call a woman honey or sweetheart, or whatever, is that right?"

His voice was deceptively mild and Mary struggled to pull herself together. If he'd just put on a shirt she might make it through the night. But she couldn't very well offer him hers, now could she? "Demeaning? Yes, I do. And so do most other women."

"Let me get this straight." Luke moved again and Mary found herself mesmerized by the muscles dancing beneath his sleekly smooth skin. "You think it's demeaning for a man to use a term of endearment when speaking to a woman, but it's perfectly alright for a woman to ogle a man's naked physique?"

"What do you mean, ogle men's bodies? That's ridiculous." Mary felt the heat rush to her cheeks. Well, damn how was she going to get out of this now?

Again, Luke's brows rose. "Is it? You mean you weren't–aren't," he amended, noting the direction of her gaze. "Ogling my chest?"

The silence stretched between them, the drumming of the rain on the tin roof the only sound to be heard. Mary darted a quick look at Luke's face from beneath the thick veil of her lashes. She knew that stubborn look. He'd sit there all night long if she didn't say something.

"Oh alright, I admit it." Anger and embarrassment vied for top billing. Thankfully, anger won. "I was ogling you. But you were ogling me, too. It doesn't mean a thing."

Luke laughed, a soft sound that drew her gaze again. His hot look killed her anger and created an answering flame deep inside.

"That's too bad it doesn't mean a thing to you, honey, because it means a lot to me." His hoarse whisper raked across her sensitized nerves. "If you look a little lower, you'll see exactly how much it means to me."

Mary's hands trembled as she reached out and fidgeted with her spoon. Only the telltale pulse at the base of Luke's throat gave any hint of his thoughts. He took the silverware from her hand and tangled his fingers with hers.

"Come here." He tugged her across the small space the separated them.

Mary obeyed his command. She heard the scrape of his chair seconds before her body met his.

Mary felt her whole body flood with joy.

And love.

It felt so good to think about it, to let it flow through her body and fill all the dark and lonely places that had felt empty for so many years. Lord, she thought, how had she done it? How had she buried this need, this longing, for so long?

"Mary?"

The look she bestowed on him answered the question as old as time itself. She knew they'd raced toward this moment since the dance. Since the day in the barn. She lowered her head and his lips met hers halfway. Their sighs of contentment mingled together.

The desire-filled kiss blossomed with their longing. Mary wanted to shout for joy and cry all at the same time. Luke broke the kiss and brushed her hair back from her face in a tender caress. She knew she would give herself to him tonight, but as he continued to stare at her, her confidence plummeted. She'd seen that look before. Rejection. Disappointment. She struggled to free herself from his grasp.

"Damn it, Mary, stop," he growled and held her in place with a bruising force.

"I've been rejected before, Luke. You don't have to sugarcoat it." After several minutes, she knew she couldn't free herself. She stopped and held her body rigid and waited for him to release her.

"That's not it, baby. I want you. But not like this." Ignoring her protest, he lifted her and carried her to the bed. He laid her gently upon the soft mattress. "All we're going to do tonight is talk, Mary." A slow, sexy grin split his face as he lowered his big body to hers. "And maybe engage in a little heavy petting."

Her heart melted at the look of intense longing in Luke's glittering eyes. She wanted Luke Tanner. Wanted him as much as he wanted her. He had been a fire burning in her blood for days, for weeks. And if she was completely honest with herself, ever since that summer camp.

And she was going to have him tonight and damn the consequences.

Fully aware of the implications of her actions, Mary shifted her weight, plunging her leg between his, rubbing against his erection.

"Be sure, Mary. Be very sure."

For only the second time in her life, Mary was completely certain about something. "I am, Luke. I am."

He gathered her in his arms and kissed her. His kiss was filled with passion. And promise. She returned the caress. She found the roof of his mouth and stroked it with her tongue. He tasted of soup and salt. All male. She heard him groan; then he became the aggressor again. His tongue moved past her lips, finding her sweetness and exploring it with a hard, questing motion. The kiss seemed to last forever.

"Your hair has driven me crazy for the past two months." He smoothed the long strands away from her face before his hand traveled down the soft fabric of her shirt. He cupped the roundness of her shoulders before his fingertips traced the burgeoning curves of her breasts. He lingered at her nipples. She moaned as he plucked them with his fingers. He started to lift her shirt but she stopped him. "Please, Luke. I'd like to keep it on."

"Why Mary?"

Mary couldn't meet his eyes. How could she tell the man who was about to become more intimate with her than any other human being on earth ever had, that she was afraid to let him see her completely naked? A lifetime of insecurities and inhibitions could not be shed with the discarding of a shirt.

For an instant, Luke's hands tightened on the fabric beneath his hand. She was afraid he would refuse her request. His fingers loosened his grip and eased up towards the neck of her shirt. He unfastened the buttons, stopping just below her breasts. "I want to see you, baby. Please let me."

Mary's eyes filled with tears as he waited for her to reveal herself to his eyes. She knew he would never force her or scold her, no matter what she decided. But she wasn't ready, instead, she pulled the flannel aside, baring her breasts to him. For an endless moment, all he did was stare. Then he lowered his head, covering her with soft, burning kisses. "God you are beautiful."

With a reverent touch, he covered one breast with his hand and squeezed the soft mound until the nipple hardened into a tight little bud "I've thought of you every night, ached for you since you came to the ranch."

Mary couldn't answer, her breath had been lost the moment he'd touched her. His hand cupped her hips bringing her into contact with his hard male form. His body was cradled on top of hers. She moved her legs restlessly, seeking his strength.

He rose from the bed and removed his jeans. His mouth was swollen from the intensity of the kisses they had shared. He bowed his head as if in prayer. She knew what was causing his restraint. Holding out her hand she urged him to her. "Luke, please love me."

He lowered his body to hers. "I don't want to hurt you."

"You won't." She felt precious and all the more desirable for his concern.

He moved his hips in a slow circular motion, letting her feel just how much he wanted her. Mary gasped at the full evidence of his desire.

"I'm on fire," he whispered. "Burning…"

"I am too," she moaned. She twisted and arched beneath him. Never had she felt such intense longing, such overwhelming sensations.

Her hand wandered over his muscled back. She snuggled deeper into his arms, welcoming his strong embrace. She had never felt so safe. "I love you, Luke. I'll always love you."

The quiet declaration didn't seem to startle him and Mary wondered how long he had known about her feelings.

"Don't make promises you can't keep, Mary," he said quietly. "Love lasts as long as the night. No longer."

"That's not true," she denied.

"We'll take it slow. See what happens."

"Okay," Mary agreed, meeting his mouth as it descended toward hers, but promised that one day she would show this reluctant rancher just how much she loved him.

Tonight she would show him with her body, and tomorrow she would tell him with her soul.

He arranged the long strands of her hair over her body. It was just long enough to hide the blushing pink of her breasts while still exposing their creamy fullness. He plucked at the rosy tips with his thumb and forefinger. Again and again he repeated the caress until Mary thought she would die from the pleasure.

She arched, aching to feel the warm sweet heat of his mouth. Obeying her silent demand, he lowered his head. The rosy peak felt the rough sweep of his jaw seconds before his lips enclosed it, drawing her deeply into his mouth. She felt a primitive tug deep in her womb as he increased the pressure.

Long moments later, he eased away and Mary groaned her frustration. He just smiled. "Stop me now, baby. If you have any doubts, stop me now."

Luke was amazed at the depth of his passion for this woman. But he would stop, even if it killed him, if that was what she wanted. He knew she was offering him more than the token words of love she had uttered. And he didn't know which touched him more.

"No," she cried. "This is what I want. You are what I want." She took his lower lip between her teeth and nipped gently.

"I'm a big man, Mary," he cautioned. "I'll try not to hurt you."

"You won't." She parted her legs for him and his questing fingers found the entrance of her body. She was warm and wet, ready for what was to come. He moved over her and pressed into her honeyed warmth, letting her body adjust to his as he joined them together, inch by tantalizing inch.

Her body stretched, expanding to accept the invasive hardness of his arousal. Reluctant to postpone the pain he knew was still to come, he applied persistent pressure and seconds later the truth of her innocence was no more.

Mary's body shuddered and a small gasp left her lips as Luke filled her completely.

"I'm sorry, baby. So sorry. I'll never hurt you again." He reached between them and stroked the button of her desire. "Just relax, sweetheart, it only gets better." Her head rolled back and forth across the pillow. He teased the engorged peak of one breast with his tongue then drew it into his mouth.

Mary twisted beneath him, lifting her hips into his. Jolts of fire shot through his body and burned away his control. He drew back and his eyes devoured the picture that she made. Her sliver blonde hair was spread across the pillow. Just like his dreams. His heart swelled, she was his, if only for the night.

Just when Mary thought she couldn't stand the sweet torture a moment longer, Luke stared to move. He withdrew until the very tip of his body remained inside of her. She groaned, arching her body to bring him back to where she wanted it the most.

He thrust inside her again and again, filling her with swift, sure strokes. Her body welcomed him home. Home from a long cold winter of loneliness and pain.

"That's it, baby." He caressed her ear with his tongue, adding to her pleasure. "Let it happen. Let me take you there."

Mary was wild with longing. She was thrust high atop a mountain, waiting, waiting so impatiently for that final step that would send her spiraling over the edge and into heaven. Just one touch from this man and she melted into a pool of sensation. She lifted her hips and moved against him, matching him stroke for stroke.

Luke kissed Mary's parted lips and shook with his own effort at control. She was so wet, so hot. He wanted to wait for the precious moment when they ceased to exist on separate plains and became one. She was open and giving and he knew he couldn't hold himself back. He reached between them and touched her, sending them both spiraling out of control.

Luke lay still, listening to the rain pound against the line shack's old tin roof. He propped himself on one elbow and watched the rise and fall of Mary's bosom with pure male appreciation. The action tightened the thin material of her shirt, molding her perfectly formed breasts like a lover's hand. His hands itched to touch her and his mouth watered to taste her. She was so beautiful, he could look at her forever. He sighed, content in a way he hadn't felt in years. After they'd made love, they had talked for hours. About her childhood, his parents, even his ex-wife.

She made him feel whole again. Luke's heart swelled with an emotion he dared not name. In the sweet haven of her loving arms, he felt he had finally found a place where he belonged. A place where he was loved.

He knew he had made promises in the dark and he intended to fulfill them to the best of his ability. Mary deserved rose petals and marriage. Babies and forever after. But doubts flooded him as he thought about taking the final step and making a commitment. Voices from the past whispered in his ear.

Easing away from the comfort of her pliant body, he rose from the bed and walked barefoot into the pouring rain. The night stood still; nothing stirred in the driving rain. He checked on Lady Jane. He'd gathered some grass earlier and fed it to her now. He'd have to tell the boys to repair the lean-to and cabin. And restock it. Apparently that hadn't been done in a while. They were lucky they'd had soup and stale crackers and a few dry items of clothing.

He lifted his face, relishing the spray of the cold rain. Mary's words from the night of the dance echoed through his tired brain and he cursed his success. Did she profess her love because of what he could give her materially? Could he trust her not be like Debbie, a woman looking for an easy out? Did she truly love him for himself and not his bank book? Could he be absolutely certain that his money wasn't a factor in her feelings?

And why did the mere thought of her betrayal threaten to send his soul tumbling into despair?

Because Mary was warm and loving. He wanted this woman beside him for the rest of his life, to share his dreams, to grow large with his babies.

"You're getting wet again." Her soft voice came through the darkness.

He wiped the water from his eyes and turned to her. He took in her bare legs visible beneath the flannel shirt and the heightened color on her cheeks. He pulled her further under the shelter and hauled her against him, tangling his hands in her hair and sealing her lips with his kiss.

When he raised his head, they were both breathless. Luke could see the uncertainty in her eyes, but refused to do anything about it. This was a night out of time for both of them. Tomorrow they would talk. Tomorrow they would speak of feelings long thought dead and buried. Of emotions that suddenly seemed so very right. But they had tonight to simply be together.

Luke slipped his hand between them, caressing her willing flesh. "Have you ever made love standing up?"

"No."

He felt her shiver and cursed. "You're cold again. We'd better continue this by the fire."

Once inside, Luke fed the fire while Mary fetched another towel from the bathroom. She dried his back with long, sensuous strokes. She slipped her arm around him and dried his stomach and chest. His nipples budded beneath her hand. "Do you like that?"

"Can't you tell?" He captured one of her hands, pushing it inside the front his jeans. Shutting his eyes, he held himself rigid as she wrapped cool fingers around his hot length. He guided her movements at first. She was a fast learner.

He clenched his fists at his sides and lost himself in her touch. He had to stop this, he knew that, but his body wouldn't obey. Just one more minute, one more second, one more stroke…

Deftly he turned around and trapped her hand between them.

Their kiss was long and hard, a prelude to their passion.

As she continued to stroke him, he captured the dark crest of one of her exposed breasts and pulled the tight bud into his mouth. He suckled each breast, sliding his tongue around each hard peak. When her legs gave out, he was there, tightening his arms around her.

"Oh, God, Luke."

"What is it, baby? Tell me what you want." He blew a breath of warm air across her nipple.

"I…, I need you."

"Where Mary? Where do you need me?"

"Inside."

Even as she spoke, his hand was moving, searching and discovering. He separated her folds and plunged two fingers inside. "Put your legs around me."

He lifted her off the floor then turned until she was supported by the wall.

With incredible ease he slipped inside her, burying himself to the hilt.

Her lips parted and he was there, his tongue plunging into her mouth in tandem with the thrusts of his hips.

Passion made him violent, desire made him rough. His hands firmed on her buttocks, fitting her to him. He stopped her instinctive response to move with him. Mercilessly, he drove into her. Her nails dug into his shoulders as he selfishly used her and loved her with his body. Again and again he pulled out, thrust, stretching and filling her. She arched her back, groaning.

"Don't fight me, baby."

As if his words had opened a floodgate of sensation, her body opened to him completely, allowing him to go even deeper. He pressed his face into her neck and felt her convulse around him. He thrust hard one last time.

Luke lowered her legs to the floor and slipped from her body. His movements were wooden. He was still aroused and hurting like hell.

"Go get dressed while I make us something to eat." He turned away. He knew she had questions, had seen his still aroused body, but she didn't say anything. She gathered her clothes and walked into the washroom, closing the door behind her with a small click.

Damn, damn, damn, he thought. He had taken her like a beast. He had felt her body straining to accept him and still he hadn't stopped. No, he had continued to stroke her, taking his fill.

He chuckled sardonically, feeling the bulge in his jeans. Not quite his fill.

Mary came out of the washroom dressed in her own clothes that had dried during the night.

"I'll make us some soup." He poured some of the water left from earlier into a pot and placed it on the stove. He kept his attention focused on the still water. It would take a while for it to boil.

"Luke."

He did not want to look at her. Didn't know if he could without grabbing her and throwing on the bed and taking her again.

"Why didn't you–you know, over there." She gestured toward the wall that had supported her only moments before.

"It doesn't matter." He knew his face closed up tight.

"Was it because of me? Don't you want me anymore?" Her voice was a small whisper in the silent room. Only the crackle of the logs on the fire could be heard.

"God no, Mary." He closed his eyes. "It had nothing to do with you."

"Then why? You wanted to. I felt you inside me, Luke."

"Just drop it. Okay?"

"I'm not going to drop it until you tell me what happened."

Luke spat out such an earthy curse that Mary blushed to the roots of her hair.

"I took you. I took you like a rutting bull. That's what happened. I could have hurt you."

"In case you hadn't noticed, I'm a big girl, Luke."

"Oh, I noticed alright." He stepped closer. If she said anything else about her size, she'd find herself over his knee. "That doesn't give me the right to treat you that way."

"Was I complaining?"

"No."

She stood on tiptoes and kissed him with an open mouth. She slid her tongue past his teeth. Her unrestrained response was all the coaxing Luke needed. He forgot his earlier apprehension and captured her lips, his tongue tangling with hers.

He stripped himself of his jeans then pulled hers down her legs. She hadn't replaced her underwear. Lifting her in his arms, he carried her to far corner of the room. The bed accepted their weight easily. His body was taunt and tight with need. But he had taken from her before. This time, he would be the one to give.

He reversed their positions, leaving her to straddle his thighs.

Luke lay still and willed himself to take this slow and easy. He unbuttoned her shirt and let it fall open. It said something when she didn't protest that he had undone the buttons all the way. He smiled to himself and savored the small victory. He enjoyed it even more when she felt her thighs relax and settle more firmly around his waist. He rubbed his erection against the entrance of her body. She felt like satin, soft and smooth – and oh so hot.

"I want to be there," Luke whispered huskily. "Deep inside you."

"I need you there."

"Then take me, Mary. Take all of me."

"Show me." She moved jerkily against his rigid length. "Show me how."

The fingers of one hand bruised her buttocks as he urged her up. He parted her opening with the other hand and fitted them together. She pushed down, he arched up. They repeated the action, in and out, again and again until he lost all sense of being. Where she went, he followed, giving her control.

His body baulked at the restrictions he place on it. The cabin was too hot, too small. He clenched the woolen blanket in his fist as she moved.

Long seconds later, Mary's movements again became jerky and uneven. She leaned forward and placed her hands on his chest, her hair a tangled cloud around them.

"Help me, Luke," she pleaded. "Help me."

Knowing her pain, sharing her need, Luke couldn't fight his release. Suddenly, he was the leader, pushing her toward the very limits of their passion. She clung to him as they dropped off the edge of the world, a brilliant flash of feeling suspended half-way between heaven and earth.

CHAPTER NINE

When Luke and Mary returned to the ranch the next morning, they discovered the sheriff of Fiddler Creek had issued a county wide order for evacuation. After almost two weeks of continuous rain, Fiddler Creek rose steadily, well on its way to overflowing its low banks. The town folk knew that the river which brought the gift of life to the fertile valley also held the power of their destruction. This had the potential to be the worst flood since the late 1800's.

As the hours passed, the crisis escalated, leaving little time to think, much less talk. And certainly no time for regrets.

While Luke helped his men move the cattle into the upper pasture, Mary drove to town. She tried not to think of the night past. Or the softly spoken promises. She hardened her heart and made up her mind to simply think of it as a moment she would cherish forever.

All women dreamed of finding that one special man who made them, and them alone, feel beautiful. Of being a warm, desirable woman who could drive any man mad with wanting. And last night, with his voice, his touch and his taste, her rugged rancher had made her feel just that. And that knowledge, no matter what the future held, could never be taken away. And for that alone, he would always have her deepest thanks and her greatest love.

Once she had reached her office, Mary boxed up her files. For once she thanked her military upbringing which made her somewhat obsessive about neatness. The important documents and records were easily found. She followed the advice of the other storeowners and moved what belongings she could into the crawl space above her efficiency apartment.

With such a small space, little of her furniture could be saved. She eyed her beautifully upholstered office chairs and sighed in regret. If she had been thinking straight she would have asked Luke to borrow a truck. But then they hadn't spoken on the ride home from the shack, or during the ensuing hours that followed.

And she couldn't justify asking Mark. He was busy helping the members of the community. Some families had generations of memories to try and save. She told herself not to mourn the loss of her things. People were much more important than belongings. She had done everything she could. She just hoped her insurance would cover the majority of any damage if it did flood.

Bending down, she lifted a box. Just as she reached the door, Luke stepped inside. She stumbled and almost fell as he took the box from her unresisting hands." Luke, what are you doing here?"

"What the hell are you doing here?" he snapped. His eyes had turned a dark green, indicating his displeasure.

Mary's mouth went dry. Never having professed her love before, she didn't know how to act or what to say. "I needed to get my records just in case it floods."

"Why didn't you get one of the hands to help?"

"They were busy. And so were you." She took her cue from him and pretended nothing had happened last night.

"Is this all you have?" He indicated the other boxes by the door.

"There are a few more things in the office if you have the room." If he had brought a truck, maybe she could at least salvage her chairs.

"Let's get what you need then I'm taking you back to the ranch until this is over." His voice held a note of steel as he loaded the boxes in the back of his covered truck. Within minutes they had the chairs loaded.

"I can't go with you, Luke," Mary said once they had finished." I promised to help at the community center. The town is going to try and build a levy along the west side where the river is the highest.

Jennifer and the other ladies are setting up a soup and sandwich station for the workers."

"Damn it, woman, you need to leave. Let the town worry about itself." Exasperation covered his face.

"I can't, Luke. This is important to me." Didn't he see she couldn't just walk away and leave her friends?

"All I understand is that if you insist on staying here you're going to be caught in the middle of town when that water decides to come this way. You're going to the ranch."

"I am not," she stated calmly.

"Oh, yes you are'" Luke stated just as calmly and took a step in her direction.

"Now, Luke." She backed away from the annoyed gleam in his eye. "Can't we talk about this?"

Luke followed her, his steps slow and deliberate. When she came up against a wall, he placed his hands on either side of her head, imprisoning her.

"I told you once, there's only one way to deal with a willful woman." He captured her mouth before she could move away, kissing her deeply and without restraint. Mary lifted her arms, encircling his neck. She plunged her fingers through the ebony satin of his hair. It was the most tender, yet most poignant kiss she had ever received.

"I've missed you," he said roughly, his breath hot against her throat. "All this time I've been riding around in this damn cold rain the only thing I could think of was how I felt in your arms last night, surrounded by your warmth."

"Luke." Her insides melted remembering the kisses and caresses they had shared in the dark of night.

"Mary?" Mark called from outside the glass doors. "Are you ready?"

Mary stepped away, her arms falling to her sides. Mark pushed open the door. He slapped his friend on the shoulder. "Man, am I glad you're here. We need all the help we can get. Did Mary tell you the town is trying to build a levy? I don't think it will hold but it's worth the try. Jennifer sent me to make sure Mary was packed and ready to leave."

"We were just on our way out," Mary assured him. She touched her braid as Luke moved away. She could only guess how she must look, her hair mussed by his caressing hands. "Isn't that right, Luke?"

"Right," Luke stated." We were just on our way out."

The town had the levy built within a few hours. No one knew whether it would withstand the force of the raging water or not. Mark had a seemingly endless supply of strength and patience and encouraged the townspeople as they filled sandbag after sandbag. Hour after hour, Luke worked beside his friend, never once complaining about the backbreaking work. He stopped only to call the ranch and order all his hands into town to help.

"You did a fine job out there." Mark complimented Luke sincerely as they walked to the heavy burlap tent erected near the bank to provide relief from the damp night air. The heavy rain punished the town as the storm grew in strength.

Luke shrugged, but said nothing. Despite his miserly reputation, he knew his duty to the community, but that wasn't the reason he was here. He looked around for Mary. When he saw her in the distance, he relaxed. He'd kept one eye on his work and one eye on her the entire night.

"I've got just one more small favor to ask," Mark continued." I need some place to take these people. None of them want to make the long trip to Newport. I thought you and a couple of the other ranchers could put them up in your bunkhouses and barns."

"Is that all? How about I butcher a cow or two and we set up a barbecue?"

"Well, that's a good idea." Mark grinned, seemingly unperturbed by Luke's sarcastic tone. "I bet Rooster would love to plan a little get together."

"Don't press your luck, buddy." He allowed himself a small grin. "Rooster would-"

Just then a shout sounded behind them. "Look out! The levy's about to go."

With those prophetic words, mass panic ensued.

Luke jumped to his feet and shouted Mary's name as people rushed by. Mary was not among them. Luke cursed and ran down the portion of the levy still standing. He moved from one mound of earth to another as the dirt collapsed beneath his feet. He could hear men behind him, but didn't stop to see who had followed.

"Mary!" he shouted again." Can you hear me?" She knelt a few feet away, but already a large stream of water separated them. Without any thought to his own safety, he started down the bank.

Mark pulled him back from the edge. "Get a grip, man."

"Let me go. I have to get to her." Luke pushed the younger man away.

"We'll get her, but not like that. Don't make me slug you, pal," Mark threatened when Luke cursed him. "Here take this."

One of the other men shoved a piece of cable with a rope attached into his hand and he helped Luke secure it around his waist. He plunged into the swirling water and it took every ounce of his considerable strength to fight against the strong current. It felt like years before he reached Mary.

"You've got yourself in a pretty pickle now, haven't you, sweetheart?" he joked shakily. His heart stopped when he realized she was buried in mud up to her waist and sinking fast.

"I thought the men could use some coffee. They looked so cold. But then the ground started moving." Between the rain and the rushing waters, they had to shout to be heard.

"It's okay, baby." His hands stroked her matted hair before he set to work. As fast as he cleared the dirt away, more fell in, keeping her trapped. Growling in frustration, he ordered her to put her arms around his neck. For once Mary obeyed without question and lifted her mud-caked arms. He braced himself as best he could and pulled with an almighty tug. She broke free.

"Let's get you out of here." He removed the rope from his waist and tied it around Mary's. He was not surprised to note that his hands shook with fear. By the time he had them on solid ground they trembled from the exertion.

"Doc Logan is ready to check her over." Mark helped them from the water.

"I'm fine," Mary assured him.

"Then let's get out of here," the preacher ordered." Everyone else is safely out of harm's way."

Luke wasted no time in taking Mark's advice and hurried Mary to his truck. In the cab the heat rose from their bodies and mixed with the cold air. Droplets of moisture clung to the inside of windows, cocooning them inside.

Luke's fretful gaze wandered over Mary as she leaned against the seat and closed her eyes.

"Could you take me to pick up my car?" She spoke without looking at him. He had convinced her to let one of his hands park it outside of town and out of danger.

"That's it woman. That's the last straw," he bit out savagely and pounded his fists against the steering wheel. "You almost drowned in the flood water about to wash away the town and the only thing you can think about is that clunker of a car that should have been scrapped years ago."

He hauled her in his arms. He needed to hold her. To love her. To surround himself in her presence.

"You're going back to the ranch. Your damned car can drown for all I care." He was surprised to hear the crack in his voice.

"I don't think cars can drown." He heard the laughter in her voice. Her small hand reached up to soothe a lock of wet hair from his brow. His Stetson had been lost in the river.

He glared at her. "You're not mocking me now are you, sugar?"

He nuzzled the exposed length of her alabaster skin. Taking several long deep breaths, he savored the smell of her skin.

"You know I'd never do that." She arched her back and the burgeoning fullness of her breasts pressed against the solid surface of his chest.

He lowered his head and took her mouth with primitive male force. Giving her no opportunity to respond or encourage, he simply kissed her.

He wanted to ravage her mouth and body, feel his tongue mating with hers. Hell, he wanted to yank her clothes off and take her right there on the front seat of his truck.

Instead he reigned in his rage and he ran his tongue across the fullness of her lips. He gave her the tenderness he knew she needed. His body still trembled from the past few minutes. The woman in his arms meant more to him than he cared to admit. Especially to himself.

He strove to control the desire she could so easily arouse. This was neither the time nor place. Mary needed a warm bath and hot meal. They both did. He placed her back on her side of the truck and started the engine. They were going home.

"What's going on? I've called all over the county looking for you." Joseph threw open the door and urged the wet, bedraggled figures inside. The warmth welcomed them like a long lost friend.

"Mary had a little accident," Luke explained as he climbed up the stairs with her in his arms. "She needs a hot bath."

"I can see that, son. Does she need a doctor?"

Luke read the worry on his grandfather's face and hastened to reassure him. "Once we get her warmed up she'll be fine. Mark's bringing some of the townspeople over. You'd better go warn Rooster and the boys."

"Luke, put me down this instant," Mary protested once Joseph had gone to do his bidding. "I can walk."

"Just be quiet," he ordered, his tone tightly controlled. He took the stairs two at a time until he reached his bathroom. Setting her on her feet, he bent beside the large marble tub and adjusted the temperature of the water. Satisfied, he rose to his feet and faced Mary. He reached for her sodden clothes.

"Now, wait just a minute." Her teeth chattered as she fought him. "Stop that this instant."

The frantic note in her voice stopped him, but just barely. "I need to, Mary. I need to make sure you're all right."

"Luke, I can't. Please don't ask me." Her gray eyes beseeched him to understand that she wasn't ready to fully reveal herself to his eyes, and on a certain level he did. But on the more primitive, possessive level, he wanted to ignore her feelings and rip her clothes away.

"Why, Mary? Why won't you let me see you? I've touched you, darling. I've held you in my arms all night long. I've loved you. Why can't I look at you?"

"Because." She bent her head, refusing to meet his eyes.

"Because why?" Luke soothed her as he would a high strung filly. He stroked her hair and pulled her closer. "Because, I might see something I don't like? That you might not be as perfect as I think you are?"

She hit him on the chest and leaned into him. "I'm not perfect, Luke, you know that as well as I do."

"Yes, Mary, I do. I also know I'm not perfect either. Do you think it was easy running around without a shirt last night? I know I don't have the body of a twenty-year old anymore. And..." He trailed off, unable to finish his sentence.

"And what?" He could hear the concern in her voice. For him.

"I'm not a young man anymore, Mary."

"You're only thirty-eight, Luke. You don't have one foot in the grave yet."

"Well, with Debbie I did." Luke released his hold on her and turned away. His fists clenched at his sides.

"What?"

"I never consummated my marriage."

"You mean, you never, well, never..." She faltered lamely.

"I couldn't." He turned back around. Someday he would tell her about his aborted wedding night and the months following. But not now.

"Well, I don't think you have that problem now, Mr. Tanner. After all, I am a nurse and last night, well, last night everything seemed to be functioning just fine," she retorted in a prim voice.

Her proper little speech wiped away the last lingering anger he held toward his ex-wife. "Well, since you are a nurse, it won't bother you to have me help you undress, now will it?" His hands reached for her blouse again.

"No way. Since I am a nurse, I'm perfectly capable of assessing my own injuries. Now get out before I freeze to death." He allowed her to push him toward the door. A small hand stopped him at the threshold.

"Luke?"

His heart flipped over at the expression on her face. "I'm right here, sweetheart."

"Thank you." She reached up on tiptoes to kiss his cheek.

"What for?"

"Saving me."

"I saved myself, Mary."

CHAPTER TEN

"It's not as bad as it could have been," Mary commented as she and Joseph drove down Main Street a week later. The older man had accompanied her into town for their first view of the aftermath. Since the flood, Luke sent most of his ranch hands into town every day to help with the cleanup. He took on the bulk of the ranch work himself. Which conveniently left little time for talking.

The crews her landlord hired were working around the clock but it would still be days before she could move back into her office or apartment.

"At least my insurance should cover most of the damage. I'll be in business again before I know it." She tried to sound optimistic but it was hard considering she wasn't. Only the small pieces of furniture she had stored in the attic and the files and chairs she'd taken to Luke's had been saved. She knew the insurance she carried would not begin to cover the cost of replacing all of her belongings.

"I need to stop at the post office and check my mail, Joseph, if that's all right."

"Of course, dear, but don't you worry about your business, Mary. Remember, Luke agreed to give you that loan."

"I can't hold Luke to his promise now. The flood changed everything. I don't know when–or if–I'll have enough customers to cover the bills." Uncertainty warred inside Mary on all fronts. Her business was in shambles and so was her relationship with Luke. Since the night of the flood, they'd barely had time to say goodnight or hello each day, much less sort out their feelings for one another. Assuming Luke even had feelings. Mary knew she did, but she had her doubts about Luke. Even though they had shared that night in the cabin and those touching moments after the flood, Luke had spoken no more of love or happily-ever-after.

Mary parked in front of the post office, one of the few businesses that had reopened. They entered the lobby along with several other townsfolk, grateful for the warmth. The cold spell that had threatened right before the storms had arrived with a vengeance and the cold temperatures hampered the cleanup efforts.

She took the mail the postmistress handed her and flipped through it absently. Bills, bills and more bills. In a moment, Joseph came up beside her.

"Mary, you need to go see that gentlemen over there." He pointed to a man behind the table where a line had formed.

"Why?" she asked, her attention still focused on the envelopes in her hand.

Joseph merely smiled and pushed her forward. "Just do it."

Several hours later, Mary and Joseph arrived home. It seemed as though fate had once again intervened in the life of Mary Carter.

That evening Luke slammed into the house, uncaring of the noise he created. With controlled, deliberate movements he hung his hat by the back door. A fine layer of dust rose into the air as he sat to remove his dirt encrusted boots. He'd worked in mud all of his life but nothing compared to the filthy grime left behind after a flood.

He used the small shower off the mudroom rather than leave a trail of dirt though the house. Under the hot spray, the tight control he'd exerted over his emotions disappeared. For days, he'd battled his nemesis–his love of Mary. The night of the flood had brought home just how much she meant to him. He knew he'd have nightmares for years to come when he remembered her at the mercy of the river.

He also knew that no matter how often she said she loved him, that once he gave her the loan, she would have enough money to expand her business and become very successful in her own right. She would no longer need or want anything from him. Of that he was certain. He only hoped that she'd feel obligated to keep him informed of the success of his investment. Through the loan he might still have some lingering contact with her.

He dried off and pulled on a clean shirt and pair of jeans. He padded barefoot to the empty kitchen where delicious smells emanated from the pots on the stove.

"Mary? Joseph?" Where had everyone gone? He walked into the living room, the beautiful view lost to him. His mind was too filled with thoughts of Mary.

"I'm in here."

Luke followed Mary's voice to the dining room. She had just put a match to the two slender candles on the table and he drew in a sharp breath as she turned around. She wore her hair down, its silken strands gleaming silver in the candlelight. The peach colored dress hugged her curves and swished enticingly around her bare legs. Her skin glowed like richly polished pearls.

"Hello, Luke," she greeted him, her face awash with happiness. "I've got something to tell you."

"What?"

"I got a loan!" Picking up a piece of paper, she raced around the table. "See, they approved it on the spot."

Luke took the paper. It was from the Small Business Administration.

"I applied about a year ago but had never heard anything from them," Mary explained. "They have a temporary office in town because of the flood and Joseph made me ask. They pulled the records and approved the loan. Of course, I never would have gotten it if it hadn't flooded. Which was awful, of course, but isn't this great?"

She paused for breath and looked up at him. She had the most beautiful, sensual eyes. They made him hunger for things he couldn't have.

"I'm happy for you, Mary." He had known losing her would hurt, he just hadn't known how much.

"Don't you see, Luke, this means I don't need your money." So excited herself she didn't see how her words stabbed at him, cutting him to the quick.

"I know." He walked to the den, unable to stand her elation, bastard that he was. She was right, she didn't need his money. And she didn't need him.

"I guess you'll be leaving then." His words were a flat statement of fact.

Mary gave a start at the harshness of his words but he didn't apologize. This needed to be a clean, quick break. He didn't think his heart could stand anything else. No matter what the poets said, it was better to have never loved.

"I guess so." She looked like an abandoned puppy and it took every ounce of control he'd ever had not to pull her in his arms and tell her he loved her.

Instead, he walked to the bar and poured himself a stiff drink, wondering if the full bottle of Scotch would be enough to drown his sorrows. "You've been a real big help, Mary. But Joseph is fine. In fact, he's convinced me to hire a housekeeper."

"Do you want me to go, Luke?"

He could see the hope drain from her eyes as she realized he wasn't asking her to leave the ranch temporarily, but to leave his life forever.

He forced his face to remain an expressionless mask and deliberately let her see the coldness in his eyes, the emptiness of his soul. "It's for the best."

"Then I guess this is goodbye."

Her voice faltered, but he didn't flinch.

"I guess it is. Have a good life, sweetheart." She'd never know how much he meant the endearment. He turned and walked away.

He felt her eyes boring into his back then he heard her blowing out the candles and her footsteps as she left the room. Fifteen minutes later the slam of the front door echoed through the house and he knew she'd left the ranch for good.

He curled his fingers around the glass still in his hand then threw it with all his might into the fireplace. He growled in satisfaction as it broke into a thousand pieces. He wanted to run after Mary and drag her back inside. He wanted to take her in his arms and shout to the world that he loved her.

But he couldn't.

While his heart told him one thing, his mind told him another. Betrayal and anger were all that he'd ever known from the people he loved. First from his parents and then his ex-wife. He couldn't withstand the pain if Mary turned out just like the others, pretending to love him until she got what she wanted.

It was better this way, he told himself. He'd done the leaving, he'd called the shots. But that didn't quell the waves of agony ripping his insides to shreds. He felt as though he had lost the most vital part of himself. The part that made him want to go on living. He closed his eyes against the pain. The look on her face when he'd told her to leave would haunt him for the rest of his days.

Mary walked through her office, her steps slow and uneven. She stopped at the small basket of ivy in her window. She'd picked up the plant the day she'd gotten the loan, a little present to herself in celebration of the good news. But its leaves had turned brown and withered. It had died as surely as her dreams.

The sun shone through the blinds but even that didn't lift her spirits. It had been over a month since she'd left the Circle T. Since she'd left Luke.

The town had gotten back to normal, the weather had warmed considerably, and her business flourished like never before. She should have been the happiest woman in the world, but she wasn't. And she didn't know if she would ever be again.

She missed Joseph. And Luke. Lord, how she missed Luke. She missed his touch, she missed the sound of his voice, she missed the sight of his tall body striding across the pasture. She was hopelessly, completely in love with the coldhearted rancher.

And for that reason she had to leave the only place that had ever felt like home.

She wiped her eyes and squared her shoulders. She had shed enough tears in the last few weeks to last a lifetime. She needed work to take her mind off her problems and she had a lot to do before leaving Fiddler Creek. Surprisingly enough, Joseph's friend Sara had offered to take over the agency. The small business loan had been transferred into her name without any problems. Mary had sworn the other woman to secrecy and made her promise not to tell the Tanners until after she left.

Mary unlocked the front door and flipped the sign to 'open'. Moments later, the bell jangled announcing someone's arrival.

"Good morning," Joseph said.

"Oh, Joseph, it's so good to see you." She rushed forward and gave him a fierce hug. She hadn't seen the older man since she'd left the ranch.

Joseph kissed her on the forehead then pulled back to take a good look at her. "I'm sorry I haven't been in before. I didn't know if I'd be welcome."

"Of course you're welcome." Just seeing her friend brought tears to her eyes. "How's Hawk and the foal?"

"Hawk's fine and the colt is the son of his father, that's for sure," he said, referring to the foal that had been born the night Luke and Mary had stayed in the line shack. "Luke named him Midnight Fire."

"That's great." Mary blushed, wondering if the colt's name had been inspired by their time together. If he hadn't thrown her off the ranch, she might have thought so. That night had been the happiest of her life, the beginning of her future with Luke or so she'd thought. But she had been wrong. Terribly wrong.

"How are you?" Worry was evident in his faded green eyes.

His tenderness almost broke through her staunch control. She stemmed the fresh flow of tears that threatened. Joseph had been so kind that she didn't want to burden him with an emotional outburst. "I'm fine."

"Right, and I'm the next candidate for president. I know that grandson of mine can be a horse's ass, Mary. It's hard for him to trust. Give him some time, he'll come around."

"How much time, Joseph? It's been over a month since he ordered me to leave." She wanted to believe the older man with all her heart. She'd thought the loan from the Small Business Administration would somehow show Luke she wanted him for himself, not for his money. Instead it had proven to be the impetus he had needed to cut her out of his life altogether. Lord, how she had wanted to tell him that she loved him that night, but the words had not come. She'd spoken them once and he had brushed them aside as meaningless chatter.

"He doesn't want me, Joseph. I'm not the type of woman he wants." She'd seen pictures of his ex-wife. She was blonde and thin. Mary might be blonde but she would never be thin. No matter what a man said or did, they all wanted a pretty woman on their arm.

She hated to tell Joseph her news, but he had a right to know. "I'm leaving Fiddler Creek, Joseph. Sara's buying the business and I think it's best for everyone concerned if I go."

"You can't do that, Mary. Talk to Luke," he urged. "You'll work it out. He needs you."

"I don't think so, Joseph." She turned away before he could see the anguish she knew must be showing in her eyes. See the doubts that had tormented her all of her life. She felt unloved, unwanted. Undeserving of any kind of happiness.

"Luke's afraid. Afraid of what you want from him."

"But I don't want anything," she cried. "I have the loan so now I don't need anything."

"I'm afraid that's the problem. Luke has always given his affection in the form of cold, hard cash or pretty trinkets. He doesn't know how to give you what you want."

"I want his heart, Joseph. I want his love."

"Exactly, Mary. Exactly."

Luke grabbed the end of the barbed wire and stretched it tautly across the post. He took a staple and hammered the wire in place.

Repairing the fence line was a thankless, time consuming job, but one that he usually enjoyed doing. He could let his thoughts wander, let himself dream. And he had begun to have such wonderful dreams. Dreams of Mary cuddled close to him on a cold winter's night. Dreams of Christmases with silver-blonde little girls and mischievous little boys.

But not today. Today it took all his attention to perform the simple task. He had a granddaddy of a hangover with a thousand little men playing drums inside his skull.

He wore no shirt in the early summer heat and sweat rolled unheeded down his back and soaked the waistband of his jeans. An annoying horsefly buzzed in his ear and he cursed as he felt its sharp bite beneath his shoulder blade once again.

But he considered the sting just reward for the pain he'd inflicted on Mary. He wanted so much to love her but he didn't know how. He didn't know how unless he gave her some tangible evidence of his affection. He could give her money, he could support her business for years to come, but he didn't know how to say the three words she deserved to hear. Apparently Debbie had warped him on another level as well.

And it was slowly destroying him.

Every evening since he'd ordered Mary off the ranch, Luke headed straight for town. Straight for the nearest bar. Every night since then he'd gotten falling down drunk. And every morning he remembered.

He remembered the taste of her lips beneath his. The laughter and the smell of her hair and the shape and feel of her as he held her in his arms.

He ripped off his gloves and walked to the flat bed of his pickup. He splashed ice cold water from the cooler on his face and shook the clinging droplets from his hair. His grandfather pulled up in the old truck the hands used to deliver hay.

Luke studied the man who had raised him, who had been his mentor all his life and his closest friend. When the owner of the local bars called, Joseph arrived and brought him home. Every night he'd shown up at closing time to repeat the procedure. All without a word of reprimand.

"Well, what are you going to try next?" Joseph asked as he ambled up beside him.

"What the hell are you talking about?" Luke demanded. He prepared himself for the lecture he deserved, knew it wouldn't change a damn thing. Luke intended to get falling down drunk again and again. It was the only way he could make it through the long, lonely hours till dawn.

The throbbing in his head intensified. He retrieved the first aid kit and rummaged through it until he found a packet of aspirin. Throwing the small white pills in his mouth, he swallowed without any water, grimacing at the bitter taste.

"The drinking isn't going to work, you know. You can't forget her."

Luke didn't answer but grabbed the wire he had abandoned earlier. Too late, he remembered stripping off his gloves. He cursed as tiny drops of blood appeared across the palm of his hand. His grandfather just kept looking at him with those wise old eyes.

"There's not enough whiskey in the whole state of Wyoming to keep you separated from what you really want, son. And you want Mary."

"Shut the hell up," Luke snarled through gritted teeth and fought the pain in his hand–and his heart. He leaned on the fence post and buried his pounding head in his arms.

Joseph swatted at the fly buzzing around his head. "You are the most arrogant son-of-a-bitch I have ever known."

"Mind your own business, Grandpa." He saw the pity in the other man's eyes and refused to meet the green gaze again.

"Are you going to throw away your chance of happiness because of pride? Mary wanted nothing more from you than your love, Luke. Can't you give her that?"

"I don't know how. I just don't know how."

"Damn it to hell and back. I could string your parents up by their heels. They didn't appreciate one thing in life, Luke, especially not you. I'm proud you're my grandson, boy, real proud. And your prissy ex-wife wouldn't have known love or loyalty if it'd bit her on her scrawny little butt."

Luke had to smile at his grandfather's tirade. He wholeheartedly agreed with his opinion of Debbie. He'd know his parents had never loved him, but he'd been lucky enough to have known that kind of love from his grandfather and grandmother. But the love between a man and a woman? His whole adult life had been filled with women he'd bought and paid for. In one way or another.

After several moments, Joseph spoke again. "I saw Mary this morning."

His male pride reared its ugly head and Luke refused to ask about her. If she wasn't as miserable as he was, he didn't want to know.

"She seemed to think you didn't want her because of her looks."

"What! She actually said that?" he shouted. He regretted the action as soon as he spoke. The little drummers in his head worked overtime.

"Not in so many words, but I'm old enough to know what women think by now. You went sniffing around her like a dog in heat, then you backed away. What else was she supposed to think? That does something to a woman, Luke. Even a strong, independent woman like Mary. It eats away at her self-esteem, especially coming from the man she loves."

"That's ridiculous. She's perfect." He ached to hold her in his arms again.

"That's what I told her."

He and his grandfather both turned as another truck approached." Hell, this is turning into grand central station," Luke grumbled. As he spoke, the truck roared to a stop and Hawk exited the cab.

"What's wrong?" A cold chill of dread shivered down Luke's spine. His heart stopped beating for a fraction of a second then slammed violently against his ribs. A busy man like Hawk didn't make the twelve-mile trip over rough terrain for just any reason.

"Doc Logan called from the hospital." He wasted no time on preliminaries. "Mary's been in an accident."

Luke's body shut down at the other man's words. His mind went numb, his eyes refused to focus and he couldn't speak. Visions of Mary mangled from a car wreck flashed through his mind. He couldn't lose her now, not when he'd just realized what a fool he'd been. He loved her beyond reason and needed to tell her.

"I told her that damn car was a death trap." He came out of his fog and retrieved his shirt and hat.

"We've got to go," Joseph's gray brow furrowed with worry." She's going to need us."

The men jumped in the cab of Hawk's truck. Luke knew the foreman would take care of the fence repair, but it didn't matter. The whole damn herd could go missing and he wouldn't care. His thoughts centered on Mary and how much he loved her.

The long narrow corridor of the hospital closed in on Luke as he made his way to the nurse's station at the far end of the emergency room. Almost immediately he spotted Doc Logan coming his way.

"Where is she?" His words were rough and low.

"What happened? Was she badly hurt? Luke and I both told her that car should be scrapped." Joseph stood by Luke's side and voiced the questions fear had frozen in his throat.

"Mary's condition is stable at the moment. Just a little fender bender, but I thought it best to admit her. They're moving her to a room now."

Luke felt himself relax, the overwhelming flood of worry receding slightly. She was fine. She was fine. "Tell me what's wrong with her. Why does she have to be admitted?"

"I'm not sure I should tell you that, Luke. When is the last time you saw, Mary?"

"About six weeks ago, right after the flood. Was she injured at the levy? Damn, I knew I should have made you check her out then." He searched his pockets for a cigarette than saw the no smoking sign at the end of the hallway. He leaned against the wall and shoved his trembling hands into his pockets so the other men couldn't see.

"She's fine, physically. But mentally, I have my doubts. Are you in love with her, son?" The doctor's question was blunt and to the point.

"Yeah," Luke snarled. "I am. If it's any of your damn business."

"Well, I suggest you put a little more enthusiasm into that response when you tell her." A smile split the other man's face but Luke just frowned.

"I couldn't agree more," Joseph echoed the doctor's words.

"Who says I'm going to tell her?" Even though he desired to do nothing more, the doubts still lingered. Even with his considerable fortune, he was still an ordinary man, set in his ways, ornery to a fault and no prize in the looks department.

"I do," Joseph's smug voice answered for him. "Because if you don't, you lose her. She's already sold her business to Sara and is planning on moving any day."

"What? She can't move. She loves it here." He remembered their conversation that day at the corral about wanting roots, someplace to call her own. She'd found that here in Fiddler Creek; he knew she had. And now she would leave it all behind. Leave him behind.

"Just go see her, boy." Joseph slapped his grandson on the back. "Tell her you love her and you'll be the happiest man in Fiddler Creek. And I'll be the second happiest."

Luke straightened from his slouched position against the wall. "Alright, I'll go see her now. If that meets with everyone's approval?" His voice dripped sarcasm, revealing his resentment at being ordered about by the two older men.

"That'll be just fine. Doc and I will just go have a cup of coffee. I'll catch up with you later. Give my best to Mary." Joseph grinned again as he and the doctor headed down the hallway.

Luke hesitated before going to the nurse's station and asking for Mary's room number. What would he say? That he loved her until it hurt? That he wanted her in his life for the rest of his days? That if she walked away, she'd take his broken heart with her?

He drew a deep breath to gather his courage before entering her room. This was going to be harder than facing down an enraged bull or breaking a wild mustang. For once in his life, Luke knew the true meaning of 'stark terror'.

Mary lay in the middle of hospital bed with her eyes closed and the white sheet pulled up to her waist. She turned as the door opened.

"Luke." Excitement shone in her eyes for one brief moment before she closed herself off to him. "I didn't think you'd come."

"Why?" Luke moved until he stood at the bottom of her bed. He didn't miss the revealing shiver that raced through her body. It gave him hope. It gave him courage.

"I didn't think you wanted to see me again."

"Why?" He held on to the last of his pride and wanted her to admit her love first.

He saw her anger quicken. This was the Mary he loved–feisty, stubborn and gorgeous. "Oh, I don't know, maybe because you ordered me off your ranch. If you don't want me, I understand. I know I'm not the most beautiful woman in the world, far from it. But I'd hoped we could still be friends."

"Damn it, Mary, I do want you."

"Then why have you been so cold and distant? Even before I left you were withdrawn. I thought you'd changed your mind, that I wasn't pretty enough, thin enough. Not your kind of woman. I've seen pictures of your ex-wife, Luke. She could have been a model." Doubt about her appearance was written across her features.

Luke scrubbed a hand across his beard roughened jaw. To him, Mary was perfection. It didn't matter that she wasn't pencil slim or that her face wasn't symmetrically perfect thanks to the knife of a plastic surgeon. He saw the beauty of her soul. He realized it would take more than a few loving whispers to show her how much she meant to him. And that didn't bother him at all. He figured he had the next forty or so years to convince this lady of his love. And he'd start now. He moved to the head of the bed.

"You are beautiful." He stopped when he heard her snort of disbelief and took her chin in his hand. He forced her to meet his gaze. "We're both intelligent adults, Mary. I can't lie and say you've got the figure of a pin-up. But I can tell you I don't want that type of woman in my bed. I want a woman I can hold on to. You've seen pictures of my great-grandmother and my grandmother. Those women had curves in all the right places, Mary. Just like you. I think my great-grandfather and grandpa were two of the happiest men on earth. Because they had women who loved them by their side."

"So where do we go from here?"

He felt as if she was still withholding a part of herself and he couldn't blame her. He'd hurt her. He knew her insecurities, and his own, couldn't be wiped away quickly but he hoped they'd find that place of love and happiness–together.

"We grow old together, Mary Carter. That is, if you'll have me." He rushed on before she could respond. "I've been a stubborn fool according to Grandfather, so let me set the record straight. I love you and I think you're the most beautiful woman to ever walk across the face of this earth. I want you by my side forever. I want you to teach me how to love. I want you to be my friend, my wife, my lover, my partner." His hand caressed her stomach, imagining his child growing inside her when the time was right. "The mother of my children."

She said nothing as she looked away.

"Why is it so hard to believe I love you, Mary? You love me don't you?"

She nodded her head.

"I've broken more bones than I can count and I've got a scar or two as well. Hell, lady, I'm no Tom Cruise in the looks department," he drawled.

"That doesn't matter." Mary protested just as he knew she would.

"So why can't I love you just as you are?"

"You really love me?"

"I love you more than life itself." Luke bent his head to take her mouth. Without words he set about convincing her that she was the love his life, the object of every erotic fantasy he'd ever have, and the very hope for his future.

The wedding took place two weeks later at the small church on Main Street. Mark officiated.

Mary and Jennifer waited in the tiny side room, making last minute adjustments to their wedding finery. Both women looked stunning. Mary had found a white satin dress overlaid with antique lace that suited her frame and figure. Jennifer, as matron of honor, wore a lavender dress that hid those last ten pounds of baby fat.

A soft knock sounded at the closed door and Joseph's deep voice came from the other side. "May I come in?"

"Of course." Jennifer opened the door and ushered him in. "I think Mary could use another familiar face right now and I need to go let Mark know we're ready to begin."

"You look beautiful," Joseph said as he took hold of Mary's cold, trembling hands.

"Thank you. Thank you for everything." She fingered the delicate pearls in her ears that he had given her that morning. They'd belonged to his late wife, Emma. "These have made me feel very special, a part of your family."

"You are a part of the family. I'm so happy for both of you. I can't think of two people who belong together as much as you and Luke."

She heard the faint sound of music and knew her father waited outside to escort her down the aisle. Despite her protests, Luke had flown her whole family in for the ceremony.

Joseph kissed her on the cheek. "I hope you have as many happy years as me and my Emma."

Mary returned the kiss blinking away the tears that threatened to gather in her eyes. "I hope so, too, Joseph."

The older man cleared his throat. "Enough of that. Now come on, your daddy's waiting and I don't like the way he's been looking at Luke. You did say he retired from the army, didn't you?" He didn't wait for an answer." Because I'd hate to see Luke sentenced to Fort Leavenworth for marrying you."

Moments later she walked down the aisle. She leaned on her father's arm for support while concentrating on not stumbling. She trembled so badly even her feet shook. She heard a slight rustling and lifted her eyes. The congregation rose as she passed by, but Mary paid them no mind.

She focused all her attention on Luke's tall figure waiting for her at the front of the church and her eyes filled with more tears. He looked so handsome standing there, waiting for her. His broad shoulders filled out the jacket of his black tuxedo to perfection and his face beamed with one of those rare Tanner smiles.

As she neared, he held out his work-roughed hand, its strength solid and sure. She placed her smaller one in his and felt a serene peace settle within her. She had finally come home. Home to her reluctant rancher.

EPILOGUE

A year later, Luke and Mary joined the line at the end of the buffet table located in the community center. Since the flood, the town had declared every Saturday night dance night. The drama had made most realize how precious friends and family really were.

Luke wrapped his arms around her waist, laughing when he had to bend forward to complete the circle. "You sure are getting big, honey."

Mary smacked at his hands and tried to loosen his hold, but he didn't let go. "Why, you inconsiderate clod. How dare you tell a pregnant lady she's fat."

Luke nuzzled her throat. "I didn't say you're getting fat. I said you were getting big."

"It's the same thing." She relaxed into his strength.

"No, it's not." His eyes narrowed into green slits even as his hands caressed her stomach. He laughed as he felt the baby move beneath his touch.

Mary watched the delight spread across his rugged features and realized he was right. It wasn't the same thing. The insecurities that had haunted her were a thing of the past. She felt beautiful. She felt loved.

As they made their way through the buffet line, Mary insisted all she wanted were the chocolate covered strawberries. She knew Jennifer, at Luke's insistence, had made extra just for her.

Once seated, he lifted a chocolate covered morsel to her mouth. She took a bite and remembered that first dance. As she swallowed she gasped.

Luke pulled the fruit away. "Doesn't it taste good? I knew I should have had some flown in from the coast but Jennifer insisted these would be fine. But they aren't ripe enough are they?"

"They're fine, Luke. I just think I'm a little over ripe." Her hands went to her stomach. The last of her words came out between short pants as she tried to control the pain that sliced through her body.

"Damn it, Mary. Why didn't you say something?" Not daring to leave her side, he motioned across the room for help.

Joseph hurried over to them with Sara, his bride of two months in tow. Mark and Jennifer were right behind them. They all talked at once until Doc Logan arrived and took charge with calm professionalism. Placing a hand on Mary's extended stomach he counted the minutes on his watch as another contraction hit.

"About ten minutes apart?" He looked at her for confirmation. She nodded her head without speaking.

"What!" The three men shouted together which drew the other partygoer's attention. Jennifer just grinned and gave Mary an encouraging smile.

Luke shook his head in admonishment. "Why didn't you tell me?"

Mary hung her head and avoided the look of censure in her husband's eyes. "I didn't want to worry anyone."

Luke helped her to her feet. "You mean to tell me you've been in labor for the past several hours and didn't think I needed to know?" His tone of voice promised they'd discuss this later.

"Actually, I've been in labor at least eight hours," she said, tossing her hair defiantly.

"Why, you little minx," he growled, his expression a mixture of fear and exasperation.

"I hate to break this up folks," the doctor broke into their teasing banter. "But we do need to get the mother-to-be to the hospital."

Once there, nurses whisked Mary away and left Luke pacing the waiting room with his grandfather. As they prepared her for delivery, Mary remembered that night not so long ago when she lay alone in the narrow hospital bed, dreading moving away from Fiddler Creek. It seemed like a lifetime ago. Now Luke stood by her side, his love clearly written across his rugged features.

"She's ready now, Mr. Tanner." When they pressed a pair of green surgical scrubs into his hands, he looked as though they'd handed him a snake. "Luke."

"I'm here," he hastened to reassure her.

Another contraction hit.

"Breathe, sweetheart, breathe." His face contorted as if he shared her pain.

Mary grimaced as the pain eased. "That's easy for you to say, mister."

Luke smoothed the hair from her eyes. "I'd trade places with you in a minute, lady. And you know it."

"I know."

And she did. No shadows lingered in her eyes. During the last year they had forged a solid, lasting bond she knew would only grow stronger with time. And love. Always love. The love they had for each other and now the love for their baby. He had made **her** life complete. But before she could tell him that, another nurse walked in.

"We have to get you to delivery, Mary. Come along, Mr. Tanner, you don't want to miss the big event."

"No, I don't," Luke grinned foolishly, his heart in his eyes for the entire world to see. "I've missed too much already."

One hour and fifteen minutes later, Luke introduced the newest member of his family, Joshua Adam Tanner, to his great-grandfather.

ABOUT THE AUTHOR

Joann and Patricia love romance–sweet, sassy, with a little heat and always with a happily-ever-after. Their stories always include that sweet and sassy heroine who can bring that alpha male to his knees, whether he's a cowboy, lawman or billionaire rancher. Working together isn't as difficult as one would image. In fact, they are often accused of sharing the same brain. They love to hear from their readers and nothing thrills them more than a (five star) review (hint, hint!) Email them at

pattymasonwriter@yahoo.com

Bookshelf

The Lady and the Law

Emmaline Conway knew only one way to deal with problems and life in general and that was to rush at them head-on. Dancing around a problem didn't solve anything–it only made your feet hurt. And she'd had enough hurt to last a lifetime.

Sheriff J.C. Duvall hadn't just been bitten by love once, he'd been chewed up and spit out. Now the by-the-book lawman wanted only to raise his daughter and live a quiet, peaceful life in the little town of Utopia, Wyoming. But Emmaline's constant shenanigans threaten his peaceful existence. Even if they can find a way to put their pasts behind them, can the solitary lawman and the fiery lawyer overcome their differences and build a future together?

The Reluctant Rancher

TOP 50 AMAZON WESTERN BESTSELLER

"Luke Tanner and women didn't mix, plain and simple."

Luke Tanner learned early on that no one cared enough to look past his rough hewed appearance and sour attitude to discover what lay beneath the surface–other than his wallet. When Mary Carter hits him up for a loan, he makes her a proposition she can't refuse.

Mary fantasized about Luke Tanner since her first glimpse of the veritable mountain of a man. She knows there's more to Luke than his bank account. Though she tries to hide her feelings, a fire burns between them. Will it end in ashes—or forge a love that would last a lifetime.

The Grinch and Miss Goody-Two Shoes

Mistletoe, falling snow and a six foot Grinch!

Private investigator Nicholas Trent hates the snow and the whole sentimental hype of Christmas. All he wanted was to finish his investigation and get the heck out of Winterfall, Nebraska, and back to the sunny beaches of California. But he hadn't counted on falling for his new assignment. The quiet beauty had a knack for melting his cold heart. But would she forgive him once she found out the secret he harbored?

Kate Harris had never met a sexier man than Nicholas Trent. Even though he'd been sent to dig into her personal life and perhaps take away the niece she'd raised on her own for the past three years, his soul-stirring kisses fueled her dreams. Would she lose more than her heart, or would she receive a Christmas miracle?

Christmas with the Millionaire Cowboy
TOP 25 AMAZON WESTERN BESTSELLER

The only thing Penny Shepherd loved more than the Rocking J Ranch she called home, was the cowboy that held her heart in his calloused hands. The only thing she hated worse than being thought of as his stepsister, was being the overweight girl that couldn't possibly catch his eye.

Ryan Jacobs felt not one ounce of brotherly love toward Penny Shepherd. And it was getting harder to pretend that he did. What he did feel was something so raw and powerful that it ate away at his gut a little more each day.

With Christmas fast approaching, will these two hearts find a bit of holiday magic?

Send Me a Cowboy
TOP 500 OVERALL AMAZON BESTSELLER
TOP 10 AMAZON WESTERN BESTSELLER

Shy accountant Katie Lenard wanted one special Valentine's Day before she grew old with a house full of cats. But girls her size didn't receive flowers and candy. Just once, she wanted someone to see past her less than perfect body to the lonely heart underneath.

She wanted someone to love her.

Tired of watching her obsess over the romantic holiday, Katie's best friend decides to give Cupid a helping hand by giving her an assignment with a man who meets all of Katie's requirements for the perfect Valentine. He's handsome and rich. But best of all, he's a sexy-as-sin cowboy who really appreciates a plus-size woman.

John Kinkaid has not had an easy life and it shows in his less than hospitable manners. Having the responsibility of a younger brother thrust upon him at the tender age of sixteen, he's done everything in his power to make sure both of their futures are secure. He's worked tirelessly to turn a failing ranch into an international success and he's kept tight control on his oil and gas holdings so that they will never again have to struggle. And he's kept an even tighter control on his emotions. John doesn't have time for hearts and flowers. At least not until he meets Katie. The time he spends with the curvy beauty has him rethinking his lonely existence.

A Cowboy of Her Own
TOP 50 AMAZON HOT
NEW WESTERN RELEASE

Marty Samuels had been cursed with plain looks and a curvy body. It didn't help that she had to work as hard as any man to keep a roof over her head. But Marty was good at protecting what she loved, including the strays she'd taken in and made part of her little family. So why couldn't she keep her heart safe from the sexy cowboy next door?

Ethan Blackhawk had been blessed with good looks and an abundance of charm. It didn't hurt that his family was rich as sin, either. He'd always been sure about what he wanted out of life–until one bad dog forced him to take a second look at the woman who could change his mind. And steal his heart.

www.ingramcontent.com/pod-product-compliance
Lightning Source LLC
Chambersburg PA
CBHW070921130626
46555CB00001B/231